WITHDRAWN

THE CLOCK

By the same authors

MY BROTHER SAM IS DEAD

THE BLOODY COUNTRY

THE WINTER HERO

JUMP SHIP TO FREEDOM

WHO IS CARRIE?

WAR COMES TO WILLY FREEMAN

DECISION IN PHILADELPHIA

By James Lincoln Collier

ROCK STAR

THE TEDDY BEAR HABIT

GIVE DAD MY BEST

WHEN THE STARS BEGIN TO FALL

OUTSIDE, LOOKING IN

THE WINCHESTERS

MY CROOKED FAMILY

By Christopher Collier

ROGER SHERMAN'S CONNECTICUT: YANKEE POLITICS
AND THE AMERICAN REVOLUTION

CONNECTICUT IN THE CONTINENTAL CONGRESS

THE LITERATURE OF CONNECTICUT HISTORY

THE CLOCK

James Lincoln Collier
and
Christopher Collier

illustrated by
KELLY MADDOX

DELACORTE PRESS
New York

Published by
Delacorte Press
Bantam Doubleday Dell Publishing Group, Inc.
666 Fifth Avenue
New York, New York 10103
Text copyright © 1992 by James Lincoln Collier and Christopher Collier
Illustrations copyright © 1992 by Kelly Maddox

Library of Congress Cataloging in Publication Data
Collier, James Lincoln, [date of birth]
The clock / by James Lincoln Collier and Christopher Collier;
illustrated by Kelly Maddox.
p.   cm.
Summary: In 1810 in Connecticut, trapped in a grueling job in the local textile mill to help
pay her father's debts, fifteen-year-old Annie becomes the victim of the cruel overseer and
plots revenge against him.
ISBN 0-385-30037-9
[1. Mills and mill-work—Fiction. 2. Work—Fiction.]
I. Collier, Christopher, 1930– . II. Maddox, Kelly, ill.
III. Title.
PZ7.C678C1 1992   [Fic]—dc20   90-49375   CIP   AC

Manufactured in the United States of America
March 1992
10 9 8 7 6 5 4 3 2 1

BVG

For Sally

Things are of the snake.

The horseman serves the horse,
The neatherd serves the neat,
The merchant serves the purse,
The eater serves his meat;
'Tis the day of the chattel,
Web to weave, and corn to grind;
Things are in the saddle,
And ride mankind.

Ralph Waldo Emerson

THE CLOCK

Chapter
ONE

WHEN I CAME HOME from school,
down the farm lane, my older brother, George, was
coming across the field where the merino ram was
grazing. It was late September, and the sun was going down into the woodlot out of a pink and blue
sky. George was carrying the ax, and I knew he'd
been out in the woodlot chopping firewood. It was
hard work, for after he chopped a tree down he had
to cut it into fireplace lengths with a bucksaw.
George had to cut an awful lot of wood, for Pa
owed money and if George cut more wood than we
needed for ourselves, Pa could sell it to help pay off
his debt.

I waited for George to come across the field to
the farm road. The merino ram baaed as he went
past. The merino ram was part of the trouble, for it
had cost a lot of money, and Pa hadn't paid for it
yet. We started for the house. "Where's Pa?" I said.
"Didn't he go with you to cut wood?"

George walked alongside me, looking mighty
grim. "Pa's gone into Humphreysville," he said. "He

heard that they had a newfangled clock at the store, and he wants to see it."

I stopped walking. "He wouldn't buy it, would he, George?"

"I just hope not," he said.

"Do you think he might?"

George shook his head. "He might. He doesn't have any sense that way."

"But he owes so much already."

"You don't have to tell me," George said. "I'm up in that woodlot ten hours a day paying it off."

George was nineteen. He was going to own our farm someday. But until Pa gave it to him, or died, George would have to live there and work for Pa. It took both Pa and George a lot of hard work plowing and planting and haying and reaping to keep the farm going, and on top of it, George had to cut wood to sell for Pa's debts when he found the time for it. It would be worth it, in the end; but it was mighty hard on George in the meantime. Of course, George being the son, it was natural he would get the farm. Daughters never got anything, unless there were nothing but daughters, and even then it would go to their husbands. That's why I was going to school, even though I was fifteen and the oldest scholar there. Ma wanted me to be a school-teacher, and I was bound and determined I'd be one. "How much would the clock cost?"

"Eight dollars."

"That's a lot of money."

"Not according to Pa. He says it's dirt cheap

for a clock like that. He says it's due to the new way of making them. Oh, he's all fired up about it."

"But what do we need a clock for, George? We never needed one before."

"I know, Annie. But that's Pa. What did we need a new gridiron for? What did we need that blamed merino ram for? Pa says we'll save a lot of time and get more done if we go by clock time, instead of the sun and the moon, but that's just an excuse. You know what Pa's like. Whenever he hears about a new thing he can't rest until he has it."

We got to the house and went on in. I could smell pork roasting over the fire, and johnnycake warming up in the oven. It smelled mighty cheerful. Ma was bending over the fire. She looked around when we came in. "Oh. I thought it might be Pa."

"George says Pa went to look at a clock."

"It better be that looking is all it comes to," Ma said. She flopped the chunk of pork over on the gridiron, and straightened up. "He's up to his eyebrows in debt as it is. If he isn't careful, he'll end up losing the farm."

That scared me. "That wouldn't happen, would it, Ma?"

She saw I was scared. "No, Annie. I don't think it'd go that far. But you know your pa."

George went over to stand in front of the fire and warm his hands. "Ma, can't you stop him?"

"George, don't bring all that up again. I've done my best." She stood with her hands on her hips, the long fork sticking out to one side. "He's head of this household and it's his right to do as he likes."

"I'm the one who's in the woodlot paying for his fancy notions."

"George, that's enough."

"I'll say something to him. If he comes home with that clock I'll say something to him."

"No, you won't, George. You're his son, you'll respect him."

"Ma," I said. "How much does he owe?"

"That's his business," Ma said.

"I have a right to know," George said. "I'm the one who's paying the debt off."

"No, you don't. You don't have a right—not until Pa wants you to know." Ma looked at George, and then at me, mighty grim. Then she sighed, and shook her head. "The Lord knows I've talked to him about it. The Lord knows I've talked, and begged, and done what I could. But it isn't any use. He can't help himself. That's Pa's way and we have to accept him for what he is." She shook her head again. "That's all there is to be said on the subject."

Then, from somewhere outside, we could hear a distant voice—no words, just a voice. We stood, listening. In a moment there came the sound of singing: "Do ye ken John Peele, with his coat so red . . ."

George and I looked at Ma, and we all knew that he'd bought the clock. Ma turned her face away from us, and stared straight ahead. "That's your pa," she said. "George, put the ax away. Annie, go set the table."

George went out through the back door to the barn, and I went to the cupboard and started taking down the platter. The singing came closer: "Do ye ken John Peele at the break of day . . ."

Ma said nothing, but went to the fireplace and tested the chunk of pork with the fork. Then the door burst open and there stood Pa. He was carrying something wrapped up in a piece of cloth under one arm. He flung the other arm out. "Do ye ken John Peele in the moooorniiiing," he finished up. He came in and banged the door closed. "Look," he cried. "You'll never believe what I've got."

Ma frowned. "Pa—"

"Don't say anything, Ma," he shouted in his cheerful way. "Not until you've seen it. It's a wonder." He set the package on the trestle table, where we ate. The piece of cloth was tied around it with string. Pa began to unknot the string. "It's a marvel of the age. The minute I saw it I knew I'd never rest until I had it."

"Pa—"

"Ma, just wait until you see it before you say anything."

"I'll wait," she said. She clamped her lips together and went on frowning. Pa got the string unknotted, and unwound it from the package. As he did, the cloth fell off. There stood a clock—or at least the inside of a clock, for it was just the works and face without a case.

Pa held his hand out toward it. "Look at that," he cried. "A marvel. The newest thing."

"Pa, it's just the works," I said.

"That's the whole idea," Pa said. "Selling it this way keeps the price down. Why, it was dirt cheap, this marvel. You see, it's the new manufacturing system that does it. No more business of a clockmaker toiling over each clock. No, sir, that's old hat. In the new manufacturing system, the job is divided up. This man winds the springs, this one paints the face, the other one cuts the gears. They can turn them out ten times as fast. Then you sell them without a case, and the price drops down to a mere pittance."

Ma looked at me, mighty unhappy. Then she turned to Pa. "You haven't paid for the merino ram yet, Pa. Don't you think you ought to pay for it first?"

He waved his hand. "I'll pay for the ram when I sell it. I promised eight hundred when I got it and I could sell it for over a thousand already. Everybody with a flock of ewes wanted to get hold of a merino ram, the wool's so good. There's no telling how high the price will go."

"Prices go down as well as up, Pa."

"Not very likely for a merino ram. Not with the demand for them that there is now. They come all the way from Spain, and there's only a few of them in New England."

Ma didn't say anything. Then she said, "How much was that marvel of a clock?"

"Eight dollars," he said. "A pittance."

Ma looked mighty grim. Eight dollars was no pittance. It was a lot of money. It'd take a man a month to earn that much. But it wasn't my business to say so.

Ma gave Pa a look. "How do you mean to pay for it, Pa?"

He looked out the window, then down at the floor. Then he looked at me, and out the window again. "I've decided," he said. "I've decided that Annie will go to work in the mill."

Ma took a gasp of air. "No," she said, mighty sharp.

Finally Pa looked at her. "Now, I don't want any argument about it. I've decided, and that's final."

"I won't have it," Ma said. "She's going to be a schoolteacher."

My heart was sinking, but I should have known it. The woolen mill was the biggest thing that had happened in Humphreysville for years. When you got down to it, it was the only thing that had ever happened in Humphreysville, for it made the village what it was. Up to now Colonel Humphreys had gotten orphan boys up from New York as mill hands. It seemed like there were plenty of orphan boys in New York—more than they had any use for down there anyway. So they shipped them up to our part of Connecticut to work in the mills. Colonel Humphreys didn't have to pay them anything, just their keep, and see to it that they got some schooling and went to church and were whipped frequently enough to turn them into good citizens. But the New York boys were a rough bunch, always fighting and cursing and stealing anything that wasn't nailed down, and even things that *were* nailed down if they could pry them loose. And finally Colonel Humphreys decided it would be cheaper to pay people from the village, or the farms in the countryside around the village, who had been raised right and weren't so likely to steal. Besides, the local people could live at home and didn't have to be provided for.

So they started hiring a few girls to work in the mills, because they'd been trained to work spinning wheels at home and the spinning machines in the mill weren't much different to work. My friend, Hetty Brown, was already working there. She liked it well enough—a lot of people did. It was pretty tedious standing at a machine for twelve hours a day, but a lot of the work around the farm was pretty tedious, too, once you'd done it a hundred times. Farm work could be cold and wet, where the mill was warm and dry; and besides, there was company at the mill, where on the farm your company was your family, who you saw day in and day out. Hetty Brown said it was mighty interesting listening to the New York boys curse and boast about stealing things.

So maybe I wouldn't have minded going into the mill; but I'd had my heart set on being a schoolteacher ever since I was eight years old. "Pa—"

"Be quiet, Annie," Ma said.

Pa looked out the window. "Now, Annie, I

know you've had your heart set on being a teacher. But we can't have everything we want in life."

But that wasn't it: it was Pa's fancy notions getting him in debt. I didn't dare say that, though. Ma said, "There isn't any sense to it. Annie can make a lot more money as a schoolteacher. She'd bring in twice as much as she will working at the mill."

Pa went on looking out the window. He was frowning and worried, and I could tell he knew he shouldn't have bought the clock. "Don't make so much out of it," he said. "It won't be forever. As soon as I sell that merino ram we'll be in the money. I'm just waiting until the price reaches the top."

It wouldn't happen. Pa's schemes never worked out. He'd stay in debt and I'd be stuck in the mill forever. But I couldn't say that either.

"Besides," Pa said, "one of these days Annie'll want to get married. She shouldn't be worrying so much about geography and arithmetic, but learning how to make some man a good wife."

The whole thing of getting married had always worried me. Sometimes I thought about what it would be like to be married—how could I be married and a schoolteacher all at once? I mean, a wife has children to care for and a husband to look after. There wasn't any chance that a schoolteacher could be a farmer's wife. There was enough to do on a farm to keep everybody busy all day long, including the little ones. If I was to be a schoolteacher, I'd have to marry somebody who worked in a shop or a mill

—somebody like Robert Bronson, who lived down our farm lane. Robert couldn't do farm work, because of having a bad foot. He worked at the mill.

"Why shouldn't she support herself?" Ma said. "I supported myself from the time I was fourteen until I was twenty-two and got married." The way she said it made it sound as if she was better off supporting herself.

It was the wrong thing to say, for Pa was beginning to lose his temper. He slapped his palm down on the trestle table. "I don't want to be argued with about this. I've decided that Annie's going into the mill and that's that."

"It isn't right," Ma said. "George'll have the farm someday. What will Annie have? The only choice you're giving Annie is to get married."

Pa folded his arms across his chest. "She'll get married. It's the only sensible choice for any woman," he said.

I sat there, feeling terrible. For seven years, since I first got the idea in my head of being a schoolteacher, I hadn't wanted to do anything else. Right from the beginning, when I was eight years old, I used to imagine what it would be like to teach school. Sometimes when I was out in the barn feeding the chickens, and digging through the hay to find where they'd laid their eggs, I'd pretend that they were children and I was their teacher. I'd say, "Now, children, don't keep moving around in your seats so." Then I'd recite some Latin poems for them.

Pooerous, abullis belartum;
Minerus, starut tucartum.

The chickens didn't mind. They'd just go on clucking around my feet, pecking at the corn I was throwing down. Oh, I can't tell you how many lessons I taught the chickens; and some to the cow, too, and even Pa's famous merino ram. But I still didn't know any Latin and had to make it up.

Sheepobo, chickogo, pigupto;
Cluckok, eatcorno, pronto.

It was my dream to be a schoolteacher, and now Pa was saying I couldn't do it.

"It's that blame clock," Ma said. Her lips were tight and straight.

Pa looked out the window. "The clock has nothing to do with it," he said. "Annie's going into the mill in order to make herself useful."

"Pa, I always did my share," I said.

"It's true," Ma said. "She did her share."

"She's fifteen. George didn't go to school past thirteen."

"He'll be provided for," Ma said.

"Annie's husband will provide for her," Pa said. "In the meantime she can do a full day's work just like the rest of us." He looked at Ma and he looked at me to let us know that he'd made up his mind and there was no point in arguing with him anymore. Then he went out to look after the merino, and slammed the door behind him.

Chapter
TWO

THAT BLAME CLOCK turned out to be a lot more trouble than just giving Pa an excuse to put me into the mill. Pa went on a rampage about it. He'd paid all that money for it, and he was bound and determined to get his money's worth out of it. It wasn't the eighteenth century anymore, Pa said. It was 1810, and things were changing. So he put the whole family on clock time, instead of sun time. The family was supposed to get up by it and eat meals by it, and go to bed by it, never mind if you were hungry or sleepy. I was usually hungry when I came home, and wanted my supper, but no, we couldn't eat until it was six, and the clock allowed us to.

Oh, it wasn't very long before all of us took to hating that clock. "It's all foolishness," Ma said to me when we were alone. "We got along perfectly well without a clock, and we don't need one now."

"Ma, how long will I have to work in the mill to pay it off?"

She shook her head. "I don't rightly know.

And if I did know, it wouldn't be my business to tell you. Besides, it isn't just the clock, it's everything."

My heart sank. "You mean I'll have to work in the mill for years and years?"

She shook her head. "Not if I can help it. Knowing your pa, there'll be no end to it. I'll think of something." Then she gave me a little smile. "Annie, the mill won't be so bad. Hetty Brown seems to like it."

"But I was going to be a schoolteacher."

"I want it for you, Annie. But now we have to bide our time."

I was mighty curious about what it was like working in the mill. Robert Bronson had told me about it, a little, but that was mostly about his own job. I didn't know what the girls did.

Robert hurt his foot six years ago. He and his father were in a field, haying. It was bright and hot —you always had to hay in the hot weather, when the hay had a chance to dry. Mr. Bronson was going along with the scythe, the blade going *slick, slick* in the green hay. Robert was coming along behind with a rake to make sure the hay was spread out so as to dry the best. The dust was flying in the air, and naturally Robert was sweating to beat anything. The sweat and dust got into his eyes. He closed his eyes and pulled up his shirttails to wipe off his face. Without thinking about it he took a couple of steps forward. Mr. Bronson caught him in the back of his ankle with that sharp scythe. It went right through to the bone. After that Robert was laid up for a while. But it never healed right. The tendons had got cut, and he couldn't raise his foot anymore. Robert couldn't do farm work—at least he couldn't do a lot of kinds of farm work, like haying. The only way he could make a living was to work in a store, or the mill, and so he went into the mill.

Because of his bad foot Robert slept at the mill in the lodging with the New York boys, but on Sunday after church he came home to stay with his family. We always walked home together, the Bronsons and us, after church. I could ask him about the mill when we were walking home.

That night I lay in bed, thinking. I slept up in the loft, up as close to the chimney as I could get my bed, for the warmth. There was a little window at one end of the loft, where you could see a patch of sky, and part of a big branch of the maple tree. I'd been looking out that window all my life, watching the maple leaves grow in the spring, then go red and brown in the fall, and disappear; watching the stars move across the sky with the seasons, never moving so much that you'd notice one night to the next, but one day you'd realize that the little constellation you'd been watching was disappearing out of the right-hand side of the window and another one was coming in from the left. My days at the mill would move slow as those stars, as I got to be sixteen, seventeen, eighteen, nineteen, twenty—before I was old enough to marry. All that time in the mill; all those days. I didn't see how I could stand it.

On Sunday Robert and I walked home together. We came along slow, behind the others, because of Robert's lame foot. Pa and George and Mr. Bronson went first down the lane, talking about money, mostly—Pa liked to talk about money. Then came Ma and Mrs. Bronson.

It was a pretty Indian summer day—the trees all red and yellow and brown, and a light purple haze in the distance over the fields.

Robert was my age, but he was full grown, and even though I was tall for a girl, he was taller by six inches. He had blond hair that lay all over to one side like raked rows of hay. It glinted in the sunshine, too, like the hay did. He had pale blue eyes that made him look sad sometimes, but not when he smiled—which he did a lot.

We walked along slow, with the others way ahead of us, and I told him all about it. "I can't stand the idea of it," I said.

"The mill isn't so bad, Annie. Especially now that they're bringing girls in. You'll have lots of company."

"Why didn't they ever have girls before?" I asked.

He shrugged. "They had all the orphan boys from New York and didn't need any others. But those boys are mighty hard to control. They don't think twice about sneaking off for a snooze or stealing food from the kitchen when they get a chance. I think Colonel Humphreys and Mr. Hoggart would rather have girls, who might behave better and tend to their work. But the main reason is that Colonel

Humphreys just brought in some new spinning machinery. They're called slubbing billies. When you work at them, it's really a lot the same as working at a spinning wheel. He figures that girls can do that real good, and boys don't know anything about spinning at all."

Colonel Humphreys was the richest man around that part of Connecticut. During the Revolutionary War he'd been an aide to George Washington. Even though that was more than thirty years ago, he was still mighty important, and had a fine carriage, and was always going off to New York or Boston on business. I'd heard all kinds of stories about those big cities—how there were thousands of people rushing to and fro and hundreds of shops with just the grandest things in them. I wished some time I could visit a big city like that, just once, to see what it was like, but I didn't know if I'd ever have a chance. Pa had been to Boston twice and New York once, and still talked about it a good deal, but the biggest place the rest of us had ever been to was New Haven, when we went over at Christmas time to visit Pa's relations. But Colonel Humphreys went to Boston or New York whenever he wanted.

Of course, Colonel Humphreys didn't have anything to do with the mill hands. They were just hired hands to him. That's what he had Mr. Hoggart there for, to be overseer, and see that the mill ran proper and the hands worked the way they were supposed to. "Robert, what's he like, Mr. Hoggart?"

Robert shook his head. "Oh, he's a hard nut, I

can tell you that. He's mighty quick to whip the boys when they get out of line. All a boy has to do is look at him cross-eyed and he'll get a whipping for it. Why, I saw him once take a shovel handle and smack a fellow so hard across his shin, it broke his leg."

"Did he ever whip you?"

"No," Robert said. "I'm not the same as the other boys, being as I'm tally boy. I'm higher up from them. It wouldn't do to whip the tally boy. Not unless he did something mighty bad, like stealing."

I knew about being tally boy, for Robert had told me before. He stood by the mill door weighing up the wool that the farmers brought to sell to the mill. And he weighed up the finished yarn that was shipped out of the mill to the customers, so they'd know how much each lot was worth. "Does Mr. Hoggart ever whip the girls?"

"Well, we haven't had any girls up till now. I don't know if he will. He might. He likes whipping people, that's a plain fact."

That worried me. Pa had whipped me when I was little, and so had Ma, when I spilled something or broke something. But I hadn't been whipped for years, not since I was maybe ten or so. "I don't think I could stand being whipped," I said. "What does he whip people for?"

"Mostly for ruining the work. If a boy gets grease on some wool, or damages a machine, he can count on a whipping. That and stealing. These orphan boys were raised up to steal, and they'll steal something as soon as look at it."

"What do they steal?"

"Anything they can get ahold of. Rum out of the stores. Apples, bread, cheese from the kitchen. If they wear out a pair of socks they'll steal a pair from another boy sooner than get another pair from the stores."

"I wouldn't steal anything," I said.

"It wouldn't be missed. There's enough stealing going on there as it is. When you get down to it, the biggest thief is Mr. Hoggart himself. Only nobody knows it."

"What?" I said. "Mr. Hoggart's a thief?"

He put his finger to his lips. "Shush, Annie. I'm the only one who knows, and if Mr. Hoggart learned I knew, he'd make things mighty hard for me. Oh, yes, he would."

I lowered my voice. "What does he steal?"

"Wool. Bags of it. Hundreds of pounds of it over a year."

That was a big surprise, all right. I never would have thought that somebody as important as Mr. Hoggart would steal. I could understand boys stealing, and girls, too, even, for I'd stolen pieces of cheese and lumps of butter out of the keeping room myself, when I was little. But it certainly surprised me that an important man like the overseer would steal. "Are you sure, Robert?"

"Well, I can't prove it. But I weigh up the wool when it comes back all clean from fulling, and

I weigh up the yarn when it's shipped out, and the figures don't tally. Oh, sure, you expect to lose some weight. But even allowing for the loss, there's too much difference between what comes in and what goes out."

I stared at him. "But shouldn't you tell somebody, Robert?"

"I'd be bound to get in a heap of trouble if I did."

"How'd you get in trouble? I should have thought you'd be a hero."

"Suppose I told somebody, and then they couldn't find any proof. Mr. Hoggart would be out to get me in the worst way. He'd do whatever he could to get even."

"But wouldn't they put him in jail?"

"Not if they couldn't prove it." He stopped walking and looked at me. "Now, Annie, you've got to promise me you won't say anything to anybody. Ever."

He looked into my eyes and I knew he was very serious about it. Robert was my best friend, and I'd never do anything to hurt him. "I promise," I said. "I won't say anything."

Then, to change the subject, he said, "Did you know that Hetty Brown is in the mill?"

"Yes. She says she likes it, because of the different people to talk to."

"You watch, a lot more girls will be coming in, at least for part of the year. What do the girls do all winter long except spin yarn anyway? With the money they make at the mills, they can buy all the yarn they need, and have money left over."

"Well, it'll be nice to have some other girls to talk to," I said. Then I sighed. "But still, it's mighty hard to stop going to school."

Chapter
THREE

MA'S OWN PA was a sailor out of
New Haven, who drowned at sea in 1793, when she
was still a little girl. Not long after, her ma died of
yellow fever. Ma was put out to live with her aunt
and uncle, but they had eight young of their own,
and didn't need another one. She was last at the
trough for everything, she always said—never had a
stitch of new clothing, but always wore hand-me-
downs that two or three of her cousins had already
grown out of, and were patched so much that there
wasn't anything of the original cloth left to them.
She hated going anywhere looking like a patchwork
quilt, for the other kids would giggle at her and
make fun, and even the grown-ups would make
jokes about how warm she must be in a nice quilt
like that, and such. She was last at the food, too, for
she sat at the bottom of the table, and by the time
she was served, the others would have got all the
meat out of the stew, and left her with nothing but
potatoes and gravy. She lived on potatoes most of
the time she was growing up, she always said.

When she was fourteen her uncle said he couldn't afford to keep her anymore, she was old enough to take care of herself. He found her a job with Mrs. Agnes Reed, who kept a dame school, where some of the families sent their kids. It was the best thing that ever happened to her, Ma always said. She didn't get any pay, except a copper cent at Thanksgiving, but Mrs. Reed liked her, and got her off the potato diet and saw to it that she had some clothes that had only been handed down once, instead of two or three times.

On top of it, Mrs. Reed saw to it that Ma got some schooling. Not as much as the other kids, for she had her work to do, sweeping and scrubbing and helping the cook. But Mrs. Reed put her in the reading and writing classes, and taught her some ciphering, too. Being allowed to go to that school was the first time anybody ever did anything for Ma, she always said. She loved going to school, and studied hard whenever she had a spare moment. "Oh, I'd have studied all day long if I could have," Ma said. "I wanted to study Latin, mathematics, geography, everything they taught. But, of course, I had my work to do, and knew I was lucky to be taught anything at all. I'd have given anything to have gotten to be a schoolteacher myself. It seemed to me just like the greatest thing. But there wasn't any chance of that."

So, with Ma talking about what a wonderful thing it was to be a schoolteacher, it was natural that I would get fired up about the idea, and I was happy to go to school. It was a whole lot more interesting than sitting in front of the spinning wheel all day long, which was what we did on the farm most of the time during the winter. There were four of us to keep in clothes. That meant spinning an awful lot of yarn, weaving it into cloth on the big loom, and then cutting and sewing to make dresses and shirts and trousers and coats.

The spinning wheel was in the parlor next to Ma and Pa's bed. It stood on three legs with a board across them like a small table. On one end was the great big walking wheel—about three feet across—held by an upright post on one side; on the other end was a horizontal rod held by two little rods on a kind of swivel. The horizontal rod led the spindle, which was turned by a belt that came off the wheel. Ma and I would take turns carding and spinning.

Carding is the really dreary part. When you get the wool off the sheep it's all tangled and has twigs and straw and all kinds of things—even old dried-up dead bugs—stuck in it. The cards are flat hard leather brushes with wire sticking up. You put some wool on one of the cards and brushed the other one over it till all the twigs and things were cleared out. This also separated the fibers so they came off the card in rolls like real curly hair. These rolls were called rolags.

I hated the carding because my arms got so tired, and my fingers would get pricked with burrs and nettles and briars in the wool. The spinning wasn't so bad. Sometimes it was even fun to see how even I could get the yarn and how fast I could do it.

What I did was stand next to the walking wheel, and reach down into a basket and pick up a roll of wool. Then I'd sort of mush one end of the roll onto the end of the yarn on the spindle with my left hand, and push the wheel back with my right hand. The spindle would start turning and twisting the wool I was holding. My job was to walk backward four or five small steps, stretching out the wool roll so it got twisted into yarn. The idea was to pull at it very evenly so the yarn didn't get too thin, or bunch up. Ma said all those steps added up to as much as twenty miles a day sometimes.

When I'd walked backward to where I couldn't reach the wheel, I'd take my three or four steps forward, pick up another roll, and start all over again. A good spinner could spin as much as three thousand yards of yarn in a day. That would be enough to knit five pairs of mittens, almost. Ma could spin that much, and I was getting pretty close.

But even with the two of us spinning our lives away, it seemed like we never had enough yarn for all the clothes we needed. Pa used to do the weaving, but now he took the yarn over to Mr. Grumble, who wove it into homespun in exchange for Pa plowing his fields.

That night, after supper, George and I went out to the barn to water the ox and the chickens. "Why did Pa have to do it, George?" I said.

"It's the debts," George said.

"Then why did he buy that blame clock?"

He didn't say anything for a minute. Then he said, "We shouldn't talk against Pa. He's our father."

That was right, but I couldn't help myself. "If he's the father, he should have more sense. I hate not going to school. I'm going to hate going to the mill."

"Maybe it won't be so bad, Annie. Days when it's bitter cold and snowing, and I'm up in the wood-lot bucking logs, you'll be mighty glad to be under cover."

It was mighty tedious though. Reading about Julius Caesar's wars or learning about foreign places, like Switzerland and the West Indies, was a whole lot more interesting than spinning wool. I learned the most amazing things—there were mountains in Switzerland where there was snow all year round; but in the West Indies a lot of the people had never seen snow and didn't know what it was.

A week later Pa took me down to the mill and signed me up. It was a cold, rainy October day, gloomy as could be, which suited me, because I was mighty gloomy inside, and the weather matched up. We sloshed down the farm lane, and then at the end of it turned left onto the road into Humphreysville. The village was in a valley where two streams came flashing down out of the hills and joined a river. The river went over a falls, and ran on down the valley through a forest.

Below the falls, just outside the village, a bridge crossed the river, and on either side of the falls were the factories—great buildings four stories high, and two hundred feet long. Each had a huge wheel that was turned by water shunted out of the river through a deep ditch, which carried the water under the wheel to move it, and then bent back into the river again. We turned off the village road onto the road to the woolen mill, which ran alongside the river. The noise was something fierce—the roar of the water going over the falls; the squeaking and groaning of the big wheels as they turned; and coming from inside the mills, the thumping and rattling of the machinery.

Inside, the noise was even louder, for the machines banged and shook and clanged. There were rows of them stretching down the full length of the floor, and at each machine were two boys, most of them dirty and wearing worn clothing. As Pa and I came in all the boys looked up; and when they saw I was a girl, they set to buzzing among themselves and winking at me. I'd never had so many boys look at me at once, and it made me feel mighty queer. I wondered how it would be to work amongst those boys all day long—would they go on winking and buzzing, or would they get used to me?

We walked down the wooden floor to the end of the mill, with all those boys still staring at me and making me nervous. In the back there was a little office with a couple of chairs, a table, and a chest. Mr. Hoggart was sitting there. He was a short man, but broad, and had sparse red hair, and a pink face and a big round red nose. Pa went in, and I stood outside looking around. I was mighty curious about the boys. I was pretty interested in seeing boys who stole and lied and cheated and cursed as if it was the most natural thing. It was because they didn't have a proper upbringing, Robert said, and couldn't help themselves. So I looked at this one and that one, trying to see if boys like that looked any different from ordinary boys; but it seemed like every time I started to look at one of them he'd know it, and swivel his head around from the machine and give me a wink. I'd snap my head away, and blush—for who knew what they were thinking?

Then Pa and Mr. Hoggart came out of the office. "All right, Annie," Pa said. "It's arranged. Mighty lucky for you, too, to be able to work inside all winter where it's warm and dry, rather than out in the snow and cold like some."

I didn't mention that it was warm and dry in school, too. Instead I said, "How long is it for, Pa?"

"Six months. We'll see how it goes after that."

My heart sank. Six months seemed like forever.

Mr. Hoggart rubbed his chin and grinned at me. "Mighty pretty girl. I'll be bound she's married soon enough, with those big brown eyes."

I blushed. I didn't like him grinning at me that way, and saying I was pretty. It was all right for Pa to say it, or Robert—I'd really like if Robert would say that; but I didn't like the way Mr. Hoggart looked at me.

Chapter
FOUR

ON MONDAY I STARTED to work at the mill. There were eight of us girls, and we were put up on the second story in a room of our own to keep us from distracting the boys. I was glad about that in one way, for it made me blush when the boys winked at me like that; but in another way I was disappointed, for I was mighty curious about those New York boys, and wanted to hear their stories and find out what New York was like.

But still, it was nice to be with some girls. I knew most of them from church, anyway, although not as well as I knew Hetty Brown. Hetty's ma was an old friend of my ma, going way back to when Ma first came to Humphreysville with Pa. Naturally, we visited back and forth with them, especially during the winter, at times when things on the farm were slow. Hetty was short and plump, and always looked on the bright side of things. If you told Hetty you weren't feeling good, she'd say it was probably something you ate and you'd feel better soon; and if you said it looked like rain, she'd say it wouldn't last long. Hetty was cheerful to be around.

All the girls worked on slubbing billies. A slubbing billy was really a machine for spinning. But instead of having one little spindle for twisting the wool into yarn, it had eight big ones. It looked like a table without a top—just a frame on legs. The spindles were at one end, about three feet from the other end. The yarn stretched from one end to the other. At the opposite end from the spindles there were two girls, each with a big basket of rolags. We worked just like I did at home in the parlor at the spinning wheel, picking up the rolls of wool, twisting them between our thumb and fingers onto the end of the spinning yarn. You had to watch out for the same things as home—bunching, or stretching too much so the connection broke. Only we didn't march back and forth by the walking wheel; we just stood in one place all day; and that was much more tiresome than all that walking.

There were some other differences too. First off, the noise. You could hear the great wheel creaking as it turned in the water outside, below the slubbing-room window. And you heard the main axle that came from the waterwheel into the mill, turning its gears and making all the belts turn that then turned the axles that went to each machine. And then every machine made its own whirring, or clanking, or banging, or humming. You had to speak up real loud to be heard.

The other big difference was the speed the spindles turned at without stopping. There would be no time out for tea, I could see that. Hetty told me that each of our machines could turn out three or four times as much yarn in a day as the fastest spinner could on a wheel. And the machine yarn was stronger and smoother than the homespun, she said. Pa was right about one thing; the wages I earned would buy a lot more yarn than I could spin in the same time at home. Except, of course, that's not what Pa was going to spend my wages on.

They rang the mill bell at four-thirty in the morning to wake everybody up. But if the wind was wrong we couldn't hear it out on the farm, so George would wake me up. George slept in the back of the house and when the animals started moving around in the morning they'd wake him up. He'd climb up the loft ladder, put his head over the top, and call my name. I'd jump up and dress in two minutes, come down the loft ladder, and grab a piece of johnnycake to eat on the way to the mill. It didn't take me more than twenty minutes to get to the mill, if I hurried.

They rang the mill bell again at five o'clock. We were supposed to be ready to start work then. At seven o'clock the bell rang again for breakfast, and again at noon for dinner, and again at five o'clock to let us quit and go home. From where I stood at the slubbing billy in the wool mill, I could see the bell tower, which was on the cotton mill. There was a clock in the bell tower, and I could see that, too, and now I knew what it meant to work by clock time, instead of sun time.

With sun time, the way we always worked before, and our grandpas and grandmas before us, and their grandpas and grandmas before them, you could rest a little when you were tired, and take a drink of something when you were thirsty, or a bite of bread and cheese when you were hungry. But with clock time you weren't allowed to get tired or hungry or thirsty on your own; you had to wait until the clock told you it was time to be thirsty or tired. I wasn't used to it.

Back on the farm Ma and me would spin all the livelong day half the winter, it seemed like. And if it wasn't spinning it was cutting and sewing to make frocks for ourselves and trousers and shirts for Pa and George. But now and again, when we felt like it, we'd stop working and rest. Ma'd make tea and we'd eat a baked apple left over from supper with cream on it, and talk. Ma would tell about Mrs. Reed's school, or how handsome Pa was when he was courting her, and I'd tell about being a teacher when I was grown up, and the eagle I'd seen the day before in the top of the pine trees.

But you couldn't do that on clock time. You had to wait until the bell said you could rest and eat and talk about things. Oh, it didn't take me but two days to come to hate that bell and that clock in the tower. But there wasn't anything to change that. I just had to get used to being hungry when I was told to be hungry.

They brought us our breakfast at the mill—
bread, cheese, and hot tea that they carried over from
the lodging house where the boys ate. But we were
supposed to get our own dinners at noon. A lot of
girls lived right in the village, like Hetty, and could
scoot home for dinner. But the ones like me, who
lived out on farms, didn't have time to scoot home,
and brought our dinners in dinner baskets—cold
pork, cold pie, cheese, bread, apples. They sent over
a boy from the lodging house kitchen with tea to go
with our dinners.

The boy's name was Tom Thrush. He was
about fourteen but small and looked half his age.
Tom was chosen for the job because he had got half
his hand clawed off by a carding machine the year
before. Some wool had got stuck and he had reached
into the machine to grab it, but the machine had
grabbed him instead. It mangled all his fingers so
bad, they had to cut them off, and part of his thumb
too. All he had now was a stump of a hand and a
stub of a thumb. He couldn't do regular work anymore, but he had enough of a hand to sweep, and
carry the tea buckets. Tom wasn't the only one
who'd lost part of himself in a machine in that mill.
There were a dozen of them with a finger gone, a
toe off, an eye out, where they'd had an accident.

We were all mighty glad to see Tom Thrush
come around, for he was saucy and cheerful and
would say anything. When he came around we usually asked him some kind of question, just to get him
talking. I was mighty curious to know what it had

been like to be an orphan boy in New York. One rainy day when he came with the tea for noontime dinner I asked, "Tom, did they make you go to school down in New York?"

"They would have, if they could have catched me."

Because of the rain Hetty'd brought her dinner. "Don't you want to learn things?" Hetty said.

He began to ladle out our tea. "Oh, I wouldn't mind learnin' things if there wasn't no work to it. I wouldn't mind it if they could just ladle it into you the way I ladle out the tea. But there's too much blame work to it. I mean, scratchin' away at the slate to learn your letters, and memorizing whole stacks of tables. Who cares what twelve times anything is? I never had twelve of anything in my life, except strokes from Hoggart's birch. I wasn't about to multiply *them* if I could help it."

"You'd better stop talking so much and get our tea poured," Hetty said. "Mr. Hoggart will give it to you good if he catches you standing around and gossiping."

He winked again. "I ain't scared of old Hoggart. I seen goblins that make old Hoggart look like nothin' at all."

"There isn't any such thing as goblins," I said.

"That's what you think," he said. "I seen one in New York one night on Water Street that was as big as a horse, with fire comin' out of its eyes and teeth like a set of knives. You'd believe in goblins, all right, if you'd seen that one. Of course, you don't see one like that every day. They're mighty scarce, that kind, and a good thing too."

I laughed. You couldn't help but being cheerful with Tom Thrush, once you got used to that stump of a hand. "Well, I don't know about goblins, but I heard you hollering like a dozen cats when Mr. Hoggart thrashed you for stealing that pie out of the kitchen."

"I didn't deserve no thrashin', neither, for it was the worst pie I ever stole. It warn't fit to eat—I give most of it to the pigs."

"You better pray he doesn't catch you again. Next time he'll take some skin off your back."

"Prayin' ain't much use with old Hoggart. He don't hold with church much."

"I thought Colonel Humphreys made everybody at the mill go to church," Hetty Brown said.

"Oh, he herds us over there, all right. The boys, the cooks, the mill hands in general. Then Hoggart he goes off to the Episcopal Church himself. Congregational ain't good enough for him. Least that's his story. But he don't go. He heads on back to the mill."

We opened our baskets and started eating our pork and johnnycake. "How do you know, Tom?" Hetty said.

He winked. "I don't mind going to church in bad weather. It's as good a place for a snooze as any, I reckon. But you take fine weather, when the sun's a-shinin', and the birds are singin', and things are in bloom—it don't suit me to be in church. I slink off to the tail end of the herd, and when old Hoggart's got his back turned I duck behind a tree, and then scoot off into somebody's cornfield and lie out in the sun for two or three hours until I figure the sermon's about wound down and it's time for dinner. Plenty of times I seen Hoggart come out of church after he's herded everybody in, and head back for the mill. He don't go to church at all."

"What if Colonel Humphreys catches him?" Hetty Brown said. "Would he discharge him?"

"Well, I wish he would," Tom said.

Then from the direction of the door there came a shout. "Thrush."

Tom whipped around. Mr. Hoggart was standing there, about twenty feet away, his arms folded over his chest. He stared at Tom, and then he stared at me. Hetty and I jumped up, scared as could be. Mr. Hoggart came charging down the mill floor. Tom turned to run, but Mr. Hoggart was on him like a shot. He grabbed Tom by the ear, and gave him a smack across the head that nearly knocked him down. Tom twisted loose and jumped back, but Mr. Hoggart grabbed him, and this time he swatted Tom across the face. Tom sat down hard and wrapped his arms around his head. Mr. Hoggart kicked him in the side. Tom doubled over onto the floor, holding onto his stomach. Mr. Hoggart raised his boot again. Then he thought better of it. He put his foot down and walked away, back toward where Hetty and I were staring down at the floor, our hearts beating fast, feeling mighty scared. He walked slowly up to us. But he didn't look at Hetty; he looked at me. He crossed his arms and roamed his eyes over me, and then he said in a low voice, "Annie, I don't want you to be talking to that boy anymore." He turned and went away.

I heard a little noise behind me, and I took a quick look around. Tom Thrush was standing there. His nose was bleeding and one of his eyes was swelling up. He was holding onto his side with his bad hand, and trying to wipe his nose with a piece of wool. His breath was coming fast and trembly, in big gulps. For a minute he couldn't speak. Then he gritted his teeth and said, low and fierce, "I'm goin' to kill him. The first chance I git, I'm goin' to kill him." He limped away, holding his side.

Chapter
FIVE

As much as I hated the mill, it was hard to stay angry with Pa, for sometimes he could be mighty jolly. The best times were when there was a corn-husking or a barn-raising, and a dozen families gathered to share out the work. Pa was always at the center of such things, laughing and singing, and raising up everybody's spirits. Not long after I started at the mill, we had a corn-husking bee. Pa and George had cut the cornstalks down at the end of August. The stalks had been lying in the field for a month now, drying. Pa and Ma and George gathered them all in, and divided them into two great piles in front of the house—six feet high, the piles were. Ma and I spent the next Sunday roasting meat, baking bread, making pies. That afternoon the people came—Robert and his family, and Hetty Brown and her family, who lived in the village on the green, and a whole lot of others. I shouldn't wonder if there were twenty of us all told. Pa handed the jug around among the grown-ups, and we divided up into two teams and pitched into that corn, each team bound and determined to beat the other one in husking its pile.

After that they set up trestle tables and benches, and Zebulon North and George had a wrestling match, while Ma and me and Mrs. Brown and Hetty brought out the supper. Oh, it was just as jolly as could be eating out there in the Indian summer afternoon, with the sun warm on our backs and the haze sort of purple against the hills in the distance beyond our fields.

After supper we went into the parlor and danced. Mr. Bronson played the drum, and Mr. Stock the fiddle. We danced reels and contredanses, and it was so tight and crowded in that parlor that there hardly was room to move. But we danced anyway until past midnight, everybody but Robert, who had trouble enough walking, much less dancing. I wanted to dance with him, but I couldn't, and sometimes I'd stay out of a dance to stand beside him so as to keep him company until he'd tell me, "Don't worry about me, Annie, I don't mind. You go and dance." So I did. I danced with everybody, including George and Pa. Pa was just the best dancer, for he made a point of learning the new dances when they came along. It made me proud to dance with Pa, because he was so good, and still handsome, too, when he was dressed up. And the whole while we danced he joked with me, saying I was his favorite girl, and the prettiest one in the room, and my brown hair was the color of chestnuts, and a whole lot of other things that kept me blushing and laughing. How could I be mad at Pa when he was like that?

We stayed up mighty late dancing, and, of course, the next morning George didn't wake up as usual, and neither did anyone else. The first thing I knew I heard Ma banging around downstairs getting the fire roused up, and fixing breakfast. I leapt out of bed, my heart beating quick, pulled on my clothes as quick as I could, and jumped down the loft ladder.

Ma looked at me. "Heavens, I thought you were gone," she said. "You'll catch it from Mr. Hoggart now, sure."

I glanced at the clock. It was five-thirty. What was the use of the thing if it let you lie in bed when you were supposed to be at work? Ma had laid out some johnnycake and pork on the table for George and Pa. I grabbed up a hunk of the cake and a piece of pork for dinner, jammed them into the pocket of my dress, flung on my cloak, and ran on out, the blowing rain pushing me along from behind.

Oh, how I wished I could stay home that day. It made me long for the days before I worked in the mill. I wanted to stay home and help Ma, because I knew it was baking day and that was something I loved. Baking was one of the things every girl had to learn—no man would think of marrying a girl who couldn't bake. Ma'd been teaching me how to bake bread in the big brick oven alongside the kitchen fireplace. The hardest part of that was the timing.

George would make a fire in the oven built

into the chimney, using wood that burned hot, like hickory or oak or ash. If we kept that going for about two hours it would get just about hot enough. I could tell if it was right by holding my hand about four inches above the brick bottom. If I had to pull it out before I got to ten, counting not too fast, then it was hot enough for bread. We'd shovel all the ashes out, put the bread dough on a long shovel and reach it into the oven. We baked bread first when the oven was hottest. We could cook for about four hours, going next to pies and last, when the oven had cooled down, we baked puddings. Ma could get the timing pretty close on sunny days by watching the sun approach the noonmark—she called it a dinner mark—on the kitchen windowsill. But on cloudy days it was all guesswork. After a few years of watching her, I got so I could guess pretty well when it was done just right—not gooey in the middle or burned on the outside. Ma didn't even use the noonmark most of the time—she just knew how much time had passed by natural instinct, it seemed. She didn't need any clock for it. And out came the bread all golden on top and smelling so good, you just had to cut off a little piece right away—just to test, of course.

And, of course, it was always dry and warm around the oven. As I ran through the icy cold rain toward the mill, I kept smelling the bread baking in my mind and wishing I was home with Ma.

I ran the whole way, dashed up the outside stairs, through the storage room and into the slubbing-billy room. Hetty was standing by our machine, waiting for me, for she couldn't work it alone. Mr. Hoggart was leaning against the wall, his arms folded across his chest. "It's about time you got here," he said in his hard voice. He looked out the window to the clock in the bell tower of the other mill. "Almost an hour late, and you've kept another girl from working. That's two hours you've cost the mill."

"I'm sorry, sir," I said, pulling off my cloak and jumping to my place at the slubbing billy. "The wind was coming wrong and I didn't hear the bell."

"That's no excuse. If the bell doesn't wake you, you'll have to find a way that will." He straightened away from the window and came over to me. "You can tell your pa your pay will be a half-day short."

I felt sunk and scared. Pa was going to be mighty angry about it. Oh, he'd be furious. There was no telling what he might do. But I'd have to confess, for it'd be worse when he came to collect my wages at the end of my contract and found out they were short.

I was desperate to talk to Robert about it. But it was hard to find a chance to talk to him, for he was busy at his job. Most of the time he was in the carding room, which was down at the front of the mill, weighing wool. The farmers would bring it to him there, and he would mark down how much they brought. The baskets would be hauled up on a pulley rigged on a beam outside a storage area next to the slubbing room. Usually Tom Thrush was up there to take in the basket as it rose to the big door in the storage area. It was something he could do with one hand.

I ate my dinner as quick as I could, and then raced on out of there to the carding room. Robert was sitting on a heap of wool eating some bread and cold pork. He looked up. "What's the matter, Annie?"

"I was late, Robert. Mr. Hoggart caught me. He says I have to tell Pa my wages will be short."

Robert whistled. "Your pa won't like that very much."

"I know. Pa's tight up for money these days."

"He always is," Robert said.

"I know. But it seems like it's worse now, Ma says. I don't know exactly the reason, I guess it's because he owes so much for that blame merino ram."

"There's going to be trouble about that, I hear. With the price of merinos shooting up so high, somebody's bringing in a whole shipload of them. The price is bound to drop."

That scared me even more. "What'll happen to Pa?"

"If he can't sell his for what he owes on him, he'll be in trouble. He'll have to find the money somewhere."

It was a mighty bad time for me to get my wages docked. "That blame clock, that blame ram."

"Maybe you could talk to Mr. Hoggart. Maybe you could plead with him."

I didn't want to be beholden to Mr. Hoggart. "I would hate to do that. I would hate to beg him."

"I don't know what else you can do," Robert said.

He was right, but I hated the idea. "I wish I could think of something else."

We were quiet. But I couldn't think of anything, and neither could Robert. "Well, I guess I'd better talk to him. Only I'm afraid of him. Look what he did to Tom Thrush."

"Poor Tom," Robert said. "It still hurts him to stand up straight." He pursed his lips. "I'll tell you what, Annie. I'll go along with you."

I shook my head. "I think he'd be more likely to give in if it was just me."

"Maybe. All right, I'll wait outside, and if he gives you any trouble you can shout and I'll come in."

So that was the way we left it. And when the five o'clock bell rang I went looking for Robert. He was standing in front of the mill, down below the pulley hanging from the carding-room window where they pulled the wool up. Robert pointed up. "He's up there in the carding-room. He came in a few minutes ago and told me to go on for supper, he had some business to do."

"He let you go early? That's funny."

"Only a couple of minutes early. He does it sometimes. He asks for my tally sheets and sits up there for a while. I guess he's checking my figures on the amount of wool that came in."

I looked up. It was dark now, and there was a low light flickering in the carding-room window. It seemed like it must be a candle, rather than the oil lamps we usually used for lighting the place during the winter when it got dark early. I took a deep breath. "I guess I'd better do it."

"Maybe he'll be in a good mood."

"I'd better get it over with," I said.

"When you go up, shut the door behind you, and I'll come halfway up the stairs and listen."

So I went on up the stairs, my heart beating fast, feeling kind of sweaty and scared. At the top of the stairs the door to the carding room was closed. I knocked.

"Who is it?" he said in a sharp quick voice. "What do you want?"

"It's Annie Steele, sir."

I heard some noise, and then the door opened and he put his head out. "What do you want?" he said.

"Sir, I'm sorry I was late this morning. I promise I'll never do it again if you won't dock my pay."

He stared at me. Then he looked around behind, as if he was checking on something. "Come on in, Annie. Let's talk about it."

I went in, and he shut the door behind me. There was a candle sitting on the floor, and a lot of wool scattered around in bags or just loose. Beside the candle was a bag full of wool with a string around the neck. Next to it was another bag, half full. Beside the candle was a small bottle of rum. Mr. Hoggart bent over, picked up the bottle, and had a swallow. Then he looked at me like he was sizing up a horse. "You're a mighty pretty girl, Annie. I hope those New York boys haven't been pestering you."

"No, sir," I said.

"They're a bunch of nasty little devils," he said. "If any of them pesters you, be sure to let me know. I'll birch him enough so he won't think to do it again."

"My ma says I'm too young for fellows."

He scratched his chin. "You don't have a fellow? What about the tally boy, Robert? I heard he was your fellow."

I blushed, and I tried to make myself stop, for I didn't want Mr. Hoggart to see it. "No, sir. We're just friends. His folks have the next farm to ours. We grew up together from babies. We're just friends."

He straightened up away from the door jamb, and took a couple of steps toward me. "Well, Annie, I hope you and me will be friends too. I could do a lot for you if we were friendly. I could forget about you being late this morning."

"Oh, thank you, sir."

He looked at me again. "I didn't say I was going to do it. I said I might. But you wouldn't expect me to forget about that if we weren't on friendly terms, would you?"

"No, sir." It was what I'd been afraid would happen. "I just hope you'll think about it, for Pa's

going to be mighty angry with me if my pay is short."

He nodded. "I expect he will be." He took another drink of rum. "You know, if we were friendly I could do a lot for you. I could even make you lamp girl."

That was the easiest job in the mill. In wintertime it was pitch dark when we started work in the morning, and dark before we got finished at night too. The factory was lit by oil lamps, dozens of them on each floor. The lamp girl had to go around and see that the lamps had oil in them, and that the wicks were trimmed so they'd burn right. And then as it got dark she'd go through the mill lighting the lamps. It was easy work, and a whole lot more interesting than working a slubbing billy, for you got to go wherever you wanted, and could talk to people and see what was going on. They liked to have one of the girls for the job, because if you gave the job to one of the New York boys they'd use it as a chance to go into the kitchen and the storerooms and steal whatever they could find.

But I didn't want to be beholden to Mr. Hoggart for anything. "I don't mind the slubbing billy," I said. "Maybe you could make Hetty Brown the lamp girl."

"Oh, you'd like being lamp girl. But I couldn't make anybody lamp girl I wasn't on good terms with." He squinted at me, his head slanted over. "Come, Annie. Robert's sweet on you, isn't he?"

I blushed again and looked down at the floor. I

hated having him talk about Robert and me. I hated him being in it. "We're just friends, sir."

"Just friends? I'll wager it's more than that."

I was still looking at the floor, and suddenly I realized that he had walked softly toward me, and was standing a couple of feet from me. I could smell the rum he'd been drinking. He reached out, clenched my chin, and raised my face up so I had to look at him. "It'd be worth your while to be friendly to me, Annie," he said in a soft voice. "There's a lot I could do for you."

I felt disgusted, and twisted my head to break loose from his grip. He let go. "That isn't being very friendly, is it now?"

"Please, sir, can I go?" I started to step around him, but he grabbed my arm above the elbow.

"You ought to try to be a little friendly. You'd like being lamp girl." He let go of my arm, and put his arm around my shoulders, and started to pull me toward him. My nose was filled with the smell of his sweat and rum, and I felt scared and disgusted. I pulled back and slipped out from under his arm. He reached out, and grabbed me by the shoulder; and just then I heard feet clumping up the stairs, and I knew from the clippety-clop way they went that it was Robert. The door slammed open. Mr. Hoggart let go of my arm and snapped around. "What the devil are you doing here?"

Then he noticed that Robert wasn't looking at him, or me, but at the two bags of wool next to the candle. "What are you staring at, Bronson?" he shouted.

Robert jerked his eyes away from the wool. "Nothing, sir. I just came to walk Annie home."

Suddenly I saw it: We'd caught Mr. Hoggart stealing wool. Did he realize that we knew?

Mr. Hoggart gave Robert a mean, hard look. Then he looked back at me. "You can go now, Annie."

Chapter
SIX

WHEN I GOT HOME Pa was sitting by the fire reading a newspaper. When I came in he looked at me, and then at that blame clock. "You're twenty minutes late," he said.

I didn't know what to say. I didn't want to talk about what Mr. Hoggart had tried to do, but I realized I'd better. He was bound to do it again, and some day it'd come out. "Mr. Hoggart kept me late."

"What was that for?" Pa said.

"He's—he tried to pester me."

Ma came in from the kitchen, carrying a jug of cider. "What's that?" she said, mighty sharp. She put the jug on the table. "What do you mean, pester you?"

"He says I should be friendly to him. He says it would do me good to be friendly to him."

Suddenly Ma was right in front of me, looking into my face. "Annie, did he touch you?"

"He grabbed my chin and twisted my head up.

He put his arm over my shoulder, but I ducked away."

Ma looked at Pa. He was staring at me, holding the paper in his lap.

"Now, just a minute, Annie—" Pa began.

"I never wanted her to go into the mill, Pa. I told you that from the beginning. And now see what's going on."

Pa stood up and dropped the newspaper on his chair. "Now, just a minute, you two. Let's not jump to conclusions. What did he actually do, Annie?"

"He told me to be friendly to him. Then he tried to put his arm around me and hug me."

Ma looked at me, and then back at Pa. "Was it because of you going in late this morning?"

Pa frowned. "Was Annie late? Why didn't you tell me?"

"Of course she was late. How was she to hear that bell over the wind this morning? You can't blame her, Pa."

"She's supposed to be at the mill on time," Pa said. "We're not on sun time anymore. We're on clock time. Did he say he was going to dock your wages?"

"He said he wouldn't if I was friendly to him."

"There," Ma said. She stamped her foot. "I won't have this."

Pa stood there, his hands on his hips, looking around the room for an answer. I could tell what was going on in his mind as clear as if I could see through his face. He didn't want Mr. Hoggart pestering me any more than Ma did; but he wanted my wages too. That was Pa, always getting himself tangled up over things. Finally he said, "Annie, you sure you're not exaggerating all this? I know you'd be mighty happy to get out of the mill."

"Pa, it's true," I shouted. "And that's not all. Mr. Hoggart's been stealing wool out of the mill. He's been doing it for a long time."

Pa stared at me, and even Ma looked shocked. "Now, Annie—" Pa said.

"It's true. Robert and I caught him. Robert knew all along anyway, because the tally sheets didn't calculate out."

Pa puffed out his cheeks and stared around the room once again. Finally he said, "Annie, I don't know what to say about all of this. I don't doubt your word, but it's hard for me to believe that Mr. Hoggart's as bad as all that. I wouldn't think it of him."

"It's true, Pa."

"Well." He looked out the window, the way he did when he knew he was supposed to do something, but didn't know what. "He shouldn't be pestering you. No, I won't allow that."

"Pa, it's true about him stealing wool."

He looked at me. "Now, Annie, you don't have any proof of that, do you?"

"No," I said. "But I could get proof if we found out where he was hiding the wool."

Suddenly Pa made up his mind about it. "Annie, I don't want you getting involved in anything like that. It isn't any of your business what Mr. Hoggart's doing down there. Probably he has a perfectly good reason for it. You don't know about these things, and I want you to stay clear of it."

Ma looked at me. "Your pa's right about that, Annie. It isn't any of your business. Just stay out of it." Then she looked at Pa. "But that isn't any reason why she should be pestered. If it happens again I want her out of the mill."

"Now, now, you two are not going to start giving me orders," Pa said.

Then George walked in, carrying the ax. He looked around at us. "What's happening?"

"Annie says Mr. Hoggart's been pestering her."

George looked at me. "Did he touch you?"

I hated talking about it. "He grabbed hold of me. He tried to kiss me."

"Annie's overwrought," Pa said. "I don't think it was as bad as that."

George stood there, holding the ax. "I heard something like that about him. They say something like that happened where he worked before."

"Now, George," Pa said. "It isn't right to spread rumors. If we believed half of what we heard about people, we wouldn't be able to trust anybody."

George didn't say anything, but he gave Pa a long look. Pa looked out the window. "I guess I'd better have a talk with Mr. Hoggart."

I knew if he did that Mr. Hoggart would come

down on me mighty hard. "Please, Pa, don't. It'll only make it worse."

Pa puffed out his cheeks. "I'll think about it," he said.

It was the same as with the clock. He'd paid a lot of money for it, and he was going to have us go by it, whether it made any sense or not. I could see where you had to go by clock time at the mill, for everybody had to start and stop together. But on a farm it was better to go by the sun and the seasons. You couldn't hay in the rain, no matter what any clock said, and you sheared the sheep when the shad-bushes bloomed, because that was how you knew it was warm enough for the sheep to do without their coats. And you planted the corn when the oak leaves were the size of a mouse ear. And you couldn't tap the maple trees by a calendar, either, for you had to do it when the sap ran, and that was up to God, and not Pa.

But Pa was bound and determined to believe that going by clock time was a good thing, and so he believed it; and he was bound and determined to believe that Mr. Hoggart wasn't really pestering me, either. Pa wasn't bad. He didn't want Mr. Hoggart to pester me any more than Ma did. But he wanted me in the mill, and so he saw things the way he wanted them.

But George believed me. After dinner we went out to the barn to water the animals and settle them down for the night. George hung the lantern on a peg in the wall, and we began pitching the old wet hay out into the barnyard. "He really did touch you, Annie?"

"Yes. I'm certain he'll try again."

"Was he drunk?"

"He was drinking rum from a bottle."

"Well, maybe it won't happen again," George said. "Maybe it was just because he was drinking."

"I'm worried."

George stopped with the pitchfork stuck down in a clump of wet hay. "If he does it again, you tell me. I'll beat the whey out of him myself."

"George, I've got to get out of that mill."

He looked grim. "I think you're stuck, Annie. For now, anyway. You'll have to endure it. Who knows, maybe Pa really will make a fortune on that ram."

I looked at him. "Do you really believe that, George?"

He grinned. "No. But we can always hope, can't we?"

George was on my side, that was true. He didn't want to see me working in the mill forever just to pay for Pa's fancy notions, any more than he wanted to work twelve hours a day in the woodlot to pay for them either. But the truth was that George figured things the same way Pa did—that it wasn't necessary for a girl to study geography and history, when she could be doing something useful to earn her keep.

But Robert was different, and I wanted to talk to him about it all. The next day at the mill I went looking for him, but he wasn't where he usually was underneath the rope and pulley, weighing up wool. I stood looking around, and then Tom Thrush came down the path with our tea bucket.

"Tom, where's Robert?"

He stopped. "Didn't you hear about it, miss?"

"Hear about what?"

"Robert ain't the tally boy no longer. He's got to work regular, just like the rest of us."

"But he can't," I cried. "Not with that foot."

"Maybe he can, and maybe he can't," Tom said. "But he's got to, anyway. Hoggart's had him loading bags of yarn onto carts all morning."

It was the worst possible job for Robert, for trying to walk with that bad foot of his under a heavy weight was certain to make him stumble and trip all the time. I wanted to see him real bad, but he wasn't around where I could get to him anymore. It was Saturday, though, and I knew I could talk to him when we were coming home from church the next day.

The trees were bare now, the sky was filled with clouds, and the air was chill. After church Robert and I came along behind the rest, and talked. "Of course he doesn't want me to be tally boy anymore," Robert said. "He's afraid I might calculate things out and find out how much wool is missing."

"He doesn't know you already did it."

"No, I don't guess he figures I'd have done that. There wouldn't be any reason for a tally boy to calculate that. I wouldn't have done it either, but I just happened to notice something in the figures one day that struck me curious."

"But you can't be carrying and hauling things," I said. "You'll fall and hurt yourself sooner or later."

"I don't guess he'd mind that very much."

I thought a minute. "Did you tell your pa?"

"Yes. He went down to the mill and spoke to Mr. Hoggart. He told Pa I'd made a lot of mistakes in the tally and wasn't up to the job."

"That's a lie," I said angrily.

"Shush, keep your voice down, Annie."

"But it is a lie. Did your pa believe it?"

"He *said* he didn't," Robert said. "He *said* he trusted my word. But I don't know. Of course Mr. Hoggart wants people to believe that I've been making mistakes in the tally, in case I should ever tell somebody about it. He wants to be able to say that I wasn't accurate in my figures, and nobody should believe anything I say."

"But we know he's stealing. You did the calculations."

Robert shrugged. "That isn't any good anymore. He has all the old tally sheets. Who knows how he's changed them? And he'll make sure that I don't see any more tally sheets ever again."

I winced. "I hate him. I hate him so." We started walking again. "Robert, we have to prove that he's stealing wool. If we could prove it, he'd lose his situation and we'd have a different overseer."

Robert shook his head. "I'm not sure, Annie.

Maybe it would be best to let things lie. We might just end up worse off."

"But you can't go on this way. You're bound to get hurt sooner or later."

"I have to wait it out for a while. I have to see how things go. Maybe something will come up."

"What if nothing does come up?"

He shook his head. "I'll have to quit and go someplace else."

That shocked me. I looked at him. "Go someplace else?"

"There's nothing for me here in Humphreysville but the mill."

"What about apprenticing to someone? Or getting a job in the village store?"

He shook his head. "I've thought about all those things, Annie. As far as the village store is concerned, Abel Fitch has got two sons coming along, and has all the help he needs at home. And who would I apprentice to? I'm not fit to work as a wheelwright for Mr. Brown, or as a gunsmith for Mr. Stock. What else is there? No, if I can't work at the mill I'll have to leave Humphreysville. Maybe go to New Haven, where there's plenty of shop work. Maybe I could apprentice to an apothecary."

Hearing that made me go cold all over. I'd always thought that Robert would be here. It never before crossed my mind that he might go away. What would I do? "If you go, I'll go with you, Robert."

He grinned at me. "I don't know what your ma would say about that, Annie."

"I don't care. I'll run away. I'll get a job in a mill somewhere and study when I can and get to be a schoolteacher."

Robert shook his head. "Let's see how things go," he said. Then we came to his house and he went in with his family to have supper.

I had to talk to somebody about it, and I decided to tell Hetty Brown. Her house was on the village road on the other side of the village green near the mill. It wasn't much out of my way, and sometimes I walked home with her, and had a glass of cider before I went on home myself. We left together on Monday at five o'clock, and as soon as we were clear of the mill I said, "Hetty, if I tell you a secret will you promise not to tell?"

"I promise. I won't tell."

"Know why Robert isn't tally boy anymore? It's because Robert and I caught Mr. Hoggart stealing wool. Robert already knew he was doing it, because the tally sheets didn't come out right. Then I went to ask him not to dock my pay for being late, and there he was in the carding room, filling a bag with wool."

She gave me a kind of scared look. "Are you sure?"

"Certain of it. The tally sheets have been coming up short for months, Robert says. And then we caught him. He doesn't want Robert to be tally boy anymore. He's got to do lifting and hauling, and he's bound to hurt himself." It made me feel a lot better to have somebody to tell it to. "But you mustn't tell anybody."

"I promise."

"Not even your pa."

But Hetty was bound to look on the best side of it. "Maybe he doesn't think you know. Maybe he just decided to give Robert a different job for some reason."

"I wish that was true."

"Maybe you can do something about it," Hetty said.

"He said if I was friendly to him he might make me lamp girl."

"See?" Hetty said. "He isn't so mad at you after all."

I frowned. "I couldn't be friendly to him if I tried. I hate him."

"You shouldn't hate anyone," Hetty said.

"Maybe I shouldn't, but I do. Look what he did to Tom Thrush just for gossiping a little. And now he's trying to hurt Robert."

I looked at her. "What are we going to do?"

She took hold of my hand and we stopped in the road, facing each other. "I'll tell my pa," she said.

"No, don't," I said. "You promised. We don't have any proof."

She thought for a minute. "How would you get proof?"

I wiped my eyes. "If we could find out what he does with the wool. He has to hide it someplace," I said.

"Wouldn't he try to sell it?" Hetty asked.

"Well, he would, we figure. But he wouldn't go out and sell a bagful every few days. He'd save it up until he had a wagon load, and then slip away with it at night and sell it a long way from here. It must be stored someplace."

"All you have to do, then, is find where he stores it."

"It wouldn't be so easy. How would you do it?"

"You could think of a way," Hetty said.

Chapter
SEVEN

THE FIRST THING I had to do was find out where Mr. Hoggart was hiding the wool. That wasn't going to be the easiest thing, for now that we were supposed to be running on clock time on the farm, Pa kept a good eye out for when I was supposed to be home from the mill in the evenings. I wasn't going to have much of a chance to wait around after the mill closed and spy on Mr. Hoggart.

Where was he hiding the wool? How did he carry it out of the mill without being seen? When did he do it? Then I remembered something that Tom Thrush had said, about Mr. Hoggart not going to church on Sunday with the boys. What was that all about? I bided my time, and a couple of days later, just after the noon bell rang and Tom was due to come along with our dinnertime tea, I slipped out of the slubbing room, down the stairs, and met Tom just as he was about to come up.

"Tom, what was that you said about Mr. Hoggart ducking out of church every Sunday?"

"Oh, he ducks out all right, regular as clockwork. He sees the boys in, and stands in the back until everybody's settled down. Then he slips out and don't turn up again until service is near finished."

I dropped my voice down a little. "Tom, I think I've got a way to get Mr. Hoggart."

He squinted his eyes at me. "I'm going to kill him when I get the chanst."

"You don't have to do that," I said. "He's stealing wool out of the mill. If we catch him at it, it'll go hard on him."

He stared at me. "How do you know that?"

"I know. He comes over here on Sunday when the boys are in church and steals it."

"You sure?"

"Sure as I can be. We have to catch him at it, though."

He thought about that. "If you already know it, why do we have to catch him at it?"

"We have to prove it. We have to find out where he takes it, so we can show Colonel Humphreys. He's bound to discharge Mr. Hoggart when he finds out. He might even go to jail."

Tom smiled. "Might he?"

"He probably would. But we have to catch him first. Somebody's got to slip in here one Sunday and spy on him."

Tom stopped smiling, and frowned.

"Now, what darn fool do you suppose is goin' to take a risk like that?"

"I thought you said you'd like to kill him."

"Killin' is one thing. Spyin' on him when he's alive and could kick your ribs in is another."

"I didn't think you were such a coward," I said.

He stopped sweeping and blinked at me. Then he said, "If you was to do it, how would you do it?"

"Why, duck behind a tree when Mr. Hoggart herded the boys off for church service, the way you always do. Then slip up here into the mill and watch to see if he comes up to the carding room with a sack. That's easy enough, isn't it?"

"You think he'd go to jail?"

"He might," I said.

Tom began to whistle. Then he went on up the stairs with the tea bucket, and I went on up after him. Well, I didn't know if he'd do it, or wouldn't do it. He wasn't going to promise anything. I'd just have to wait to find out.

I didn't have a chance to talk to Robert until Sunday service. Mr. Hoggart was keeping him busy packing yarn and loading it to be shipped out, and I never saw Robert until Sunday. But on Sunday I told him.

We had two services, a morning service and an afternoon one. Between them we had a big Sunday dinner. All of us who had to travel some distance carried big dinner baskets and ate together.

During the good weather we generally ate Sunday dinner outside, sitting under trees, or on the stone walls. But now it had come late fall, and the air was getting chill, we ate in the carriage shed on the trestle tables the men would set up after the morning service. The women would all bring food from home—pieces of roast pork, big pots of baked beans, johnnycake, fried squash, jellies, pickles. It was mighty pleasant sitting down to dinner with so many together in that big shed, the chickens pecking around for bits of corn bread that were dropped, and the dogs snoozing by the table.

I couldn't talk to Robert until we were done eating. Then we went outside and sat on a stone wall, the way we usually did. Robert looked tired and pale. Mr. Hoggart was wearing him out.

"Robert, I know how Mr. Hoggart is stealing the wool. He does it on Sunday, when everybody's at church service."

He looked at me. "How do you know that?"

"He doesn't always stay at service. Tom Thrush told me. He herds the boys over to our church, and then he slips off like he's going to the Episcopal Church. I'm sure he goes back to the mill and takes some wool then."

He shook his head. "You can't be sure of that."

"I aim to find out," I said.

He frowned down at the dead grass. "You're going to get yourself in a peck of trouble."

"I'll be careful. Anyway, I'm not going to do it myself. I talked Tom Thrush into doing it. Maybe."

"I wish you'd drop it, Annie."

"I can't. We have to get rid of him."

On Monday, just after breakfast, Tom Thrush came idling by, pushing the broom with his bad hand. He began to sweep around my machine. "I done it, Miss Annie," he said. "I done it just like you said. I seen him do it."

I was excited. I wished I could run out of there, sit down with Tom and hear all about it. "What did he do? How did he do it?"

"Shush," he said.

I lowered my voice. "Tell me."

"Well, I slipped behind a tree, the way I always done, and as soon as they was safe inside the church I ran on back to the mill, and hid out in the slubbing room in the shadows behind the machines."

"Were you scared?"

"Not a bit of it. He don't scare me."

"It would have scared me," I said. "Then what?"

"Well, I waited, and by and by I heard footsteps on the stairs a-headin' for the carding room. Oh, that was mighty scary."

"I thought you said you weren't afraid of Mr. Hoggart."

"Oh, what I meant to say was, it just gave me a start when he come along sudden like that. I wasn't what you would call scairt. It just gave me a start."

"Oh," I said.

"So I set there a-waitin', and after a bit I heard him shufflin' and bumpin' around in that there carding room, like he was loadin' up a bag of wool."

"And you crept over to the door and peeked through the crack," I said.

Tom blinked. "What kind of a blame fool do you think I am? I was shakin' enough just crouched down by the machines."

That worried me. It wasn't going to be much use if he didn't see who was in that carding room. "I thought you said you weren't scared, only got a little start."

"Oh, yes, that's about the size of it. I wasn't scairt, that wasn't it at all. Just nerved up a little."

"I suppose so," I said. "Then what?"

"Well, he went on bangin' and bumpin' around in there for a while, and then I heard his footsteps goin' on down the stairs."

"And you jumped out and followed him to see where he went."

Tom blinked again. "Why, Miss Annie, what on earth are you thinkin' of? I could hardly stand up, my legs was so trembly, to say nothin' of followin' him anywheres."

It had all been a waste.

"So you don't know for sure that it was him?"

He blinked one more time. "Why, Miss Annie, who do you suppose it was?"

That was true enough—it had to be him. Nobody else would have dared to steal anything from there. But it wasn't any use—I had to know for sure, and I had to know where he was hiding the wool once he took it out of the mill. "Well, Tom, that's a mighty big help anyway. I expect we'll get him sooner or later."

I knew now that I would have to do it myself. I should have known that Tom would mess it up some way. He'd spent all of his life being whipped and shouted at, and pushed here and there, and it had taken a lot of the heart out of him. He wanted to kill Mr. Hoggart—dreamed about it half the day, I reckoned—but it wasn't likely he'd actually do it.

Chapter
EIGHT

THE NEXT SUNDAY the first snow came, light flakes dancing down onto the hard, dry ground. We walked to church with it blowing in our faces. "It's going to pile up," George said. "I can feel it."

"What we need is a sleigh," Pa suddenly said. "Go to church in style and comfort."

Ma gave him a look. "Best to get a horse first, I shouldn't wonder."

"Yes," Pa said. "Now that you mention it, I've got my eye on one. Edmund Wilkins has a fine animal he wants to sell. I think I might just do it. A first-rate saddle horse."

I didn't pay any attention. That was just Pa talking. We'd walked to church through snow and rain and heat and cold all my life and it didn't seem likely it would ever be any different. I looked straight out at the snow dancing down. I liked it when the first snow came. Winter was hard, what with the cold coming through the walls of the house —so that you'd only be warm if you sat close to the

fire—and traipsing around outside with your shoes
wet through to the skin, and your hands red and
chilled. But the first snow was always pretty. As
soon as it piled up enough we'd get out sleds and go
up the hill behind the Bronsons' house to play Running the Gauntlet. Some of us would go up top with
the sleds and come down lickety-split, skidding and
sliding this way and that. The rest of us would line
up along the way with sticks, and try to tip the sleds
over as they came shooting by. I liked it when the
first snow came.

It snowed right on through the morning, but it
began to taper off around noon, when we were all
gathered in the church barn eating our dinners, and
by the time the second service ended it had stopped
snowing. But it had come down hard, and there was
a good foot of snow on the ground, and drifts two
feet deep in places. We stood out front of the church
looking at it, nothing but white on the fields as far as
we could see, crisscrossed with stone walls. Here and
there was a piece of woods, fat black lines against the
snow. Dusk was coming and the color was going out
of the world, leaving it all black and white. "I don't
see any point in Annie's trudging home through this
now and turning around tomorrow morning to go
through it again to get to the mill," Ma said. "Why
don't you spend the night at Hetty Brown's?"

Well, I liked that idea. But the Browns had
already started off for home, so I said good-bye and

set off after them, going as quick as I could up the road in hopes of catching up with them. It was getting pretty dark now, but some horses had gone along the road, and a couple of sleighs, as well as people walking, and the snow had got packed down some, and it was easy enough going. Up ahead I could see little bits of light coming from the mills and the lodging houses, and beyond that other bits of light from the houses around the village green. I kept on walking, and by and by I came to where the mill road turned off, to run alongside the creek to the two mills facing each other on the banks.

Something flashed across my mind, and I stopped walking. I looked down the mill road, taking it all in—the snowy mill road with a couple of lines of footprints going along it, the river black as tar, and the dark mills, silent except for the creaking and groaning of the waterwheels.

My heart began to beat fast. How much time did I have? The Browns didn't know I was supposed to be catching up with them. They wouldn't think anything if I was a little late getting there, for they weren't expecting me anyway. I took a deep breath, and then I began to trot down the mill road toward the mill. In a minute I came up to the front of the mill. I dashed around the side, heading toward the back. At the corner, right near the long stairs coming down the back, I stopped and looked out. Out back was the mill woodlot. Between the mill and the woodlot was a meadow about a hundred yards across. The meadow was a white blanket. It was untouched, except for a path of footprints running through the snow out to the woodlot. Mr. Hoggart had been out there at least twice, as much as I could tell from the footprints in the dusk.

I knew I had to get to the Browns' house soon, or they'd wonder why it had taken so long to come from church. I looked out across the white field with the line of footprints running across it. It was the best chance I'd ever get. So I took another deep breath and began to run across the white field in the moonlight, trying to step in the old footprints as much as I could, so it wouldn't seem that anybody had followed them.

I felt naked and scared. It was still light enough so you could see a person against the snow. Mr. Hoggart didn't live in the mill. He had his own house down the road a ways. But there was no telling where he might be, and if he looked out a window onto the field where I was, he'd know in two seconds who it was running along his footprints.

I kept on running. The woods came closer. I could see a good ways into them. I ran on, and then I plunged in among the trees. I was a lot safer there. I went in about six steps, stopped, and looked back. There was no sign of a human being, nobody anywhere. I caught my breath, and then I plunged on, following the footprints where they led. Now I was deep in the woodlot. On I went, and within a couple of minutes, I began to see through the trees a shadowy square.

I slowed down, and then stopped and squinted

my eyes to look ahead. It was a shed or a cabin. I began to move forward again, now slipping carefully from tree to tree. In a moment I came to the cabin. It looked like a large tool shed of some kind. There were no windows, and only a small door shut tight. I slipped around behind it. Still no windows, and no windows on the other side either. I guess it had been built as a shed for woodcutters to lock their tools in when they went home at night. You could store a fair amount of wool in it too.

I stood there, wondering how I could get a look in it to see if there really was wool in it, when I heard a thump, and a bang from inside. I jumped, and then froze still, my heart racing. I listened. There was another thump and a curse. I turned to run, about to head off through the woods by the shortest distance to the road. Just as I put my foot down, I remembered: I'd make a track of footprints as clear as day going out of there. He'd know somebody had been outside while he was in there.

Should I wait until he left? No, I couldn't do that, for I'd already made a track of prints all the way around the shack. There was only one thing to do. I began to run off the way I'd come, along the old footprints. And what would happen if he came out right behind me? He wouldn't be running. He'd be coming along easy; but would he get to the edge of the woods before I got across the field? I began to pray.

Then I came to the edge of the woods. I turned around to listen. It seemed to me I heard the sound of a door shutting, and a key clinking. I dashed out of the woods into the snowy field, moving my legs as fast as I could go, faster and faster along that line of footprints. The mill came closer; I plunged for it, dove around the corner, and dropped flat into the snow. Then I twisted around and looked back. Mr. Hoggart was just coming out of the woods. I didn't wait, but ran on down the length of the mill, out the mill road, and onto the village road.

Had he seen me? I didn't know. He'd have only got a glimpse of me, but that might have been enough. I didn't think he could have seen who it was diving around that corner. But if he'd seen someone spying on him, he'd have a pretty good guess as to who it was. I ran off to Hetty Brown's house as quick as I could manage.

But Mr. Hoggart didn't come around for a couple of days, and I rested easier. In the meanwhile, I got a chance to talk to Robert. Mr. Hoggart had got him carrying yarn down out of our part of the mill, and sometimes he could swing through the slubbing room and talk to me. He looked dreadful; it was hard enough for him to get up and down a flight of stairs by himself, much less carrying a huge bundle of yarn. "He's trying to kill you," I said. "He wants to work you to death."

"It isn't as bad as all that," Robert said. "I'm getting used to it."

"He thinks I'm sweet on you, and he's afraid of

what you might know from being tally boy. He wants to kill you."

"Don't exaggerate, Annie. It isn't that bad. He wants me to quit."

"Maybe," I said. "Anyway, I found out where he's hiding the wool."

"What?"

So I told him the whole story, of seeing the footprints through the snow behind the mill, and tracking them to the shack in the woods.

"That was a foolish risk, Annie. He'd have beaten the daylights out of you if he'd caught you. He might have killed you."

"I know," I said. "I was almighty scared. I was plain lucky that he didn't come bursting out of that shed while I was standing there."

"You sure were," he said. I was feeling sort of proud of myself, for it was a brave thing to do, even if it was foolish.

"Now we know where he's got the wool. We can tell Colonel Humphreys."

He thought about it for a minute. "But you didn't actually see it. You didn't get a look inside."

"No, that's true." I stood there, thinking. "But it has to be in there. What else would he be going out to that cabin for in the dead of winter?"

"Yes, that's true. But suppose we can somehow get Colonel Humphreys to look into it. What if there's no wool in it? What if he'd cleared the wool out? What if he was using the shed for something else in the first place?"

Well, it was a puzzle. Robert said we'd better think about it for a few days first, before we did anything. So I went on home. But I was feeling a lot better, because I knew Robert would help me, and with Robert I knew I had a chance.

Then, a few days later, Mr. Hoggart came after me. It was quitting time, getting dark outside. The bell had just rung, and the girls were putting on their caps and the boys were pushing and jostling to go across to their lodgings and get their suppers. I was putting on my cap, too, and thinking about my own supper, although I knew I wouldn't get it until six, for Pa was still running everything by the clock. I saw Mr. Hoggart pushing his way through the mob of boys going out. He was heading right toward me, and I jumped under my skin. Quickly I slipped into my coat, and started for the door with the others, hoping to skirt around him. But the next thing I knew he was standing dead in front of me. I tried to skip around him, like I didn't realize he wanted me, but he grabbed my arm. "Hold up, Annie," he said, kind of rough. "I want to talk to you."

"Yes, sir," I said. I kept my eyes down so as not to encourage him.

He stood there holding my arm like that until the boys and girls had all filed out and were clumping down the outside stairs. Then he said, "Look at me."

I flicked my eyes upward for a second, and then down again.

"I said look at me." He let go of my arm, grabbed hold of my chin and twisted my face upward. My heart was going fast.

"I saw you talking with that dirty little Tom Thrush the other day," he said.

What had he overheard? "Yes, sir, I might have been talking to him."

He gave my chin a little shake. "I hope you haven't been fooling around with him, Annie."

Mr. Hoggart should have known better than that. "No, sir. All we ever did was talk a little."

He shook my face again. "You sure of that?"

"Yes, sir. My ma warned me against those boys."

"A good thing too. You see that you obey your ma. I can tell you're not the kind who'd have anything to do with those New York boys. You need a better sort of fellow."

I didn't say anything, for I knew what he meant by that.

He shook me again. "What do you say to that?"

"My ma says I'm too young for fellows."

"Oh, come," he said. "You're fifteen, aren't you? You're not a girl anymore. You're a woman. You're a woman and can do the things that women do."

"Please, sir, I have to get home."

"They'll wait for you." He let go of my chin.

"Now, Annie, you know I could do you a lot of good around the mill. Being the lamp girl is a much nicer job than working a slubbing billy."

I looked down and didn't say anything. Suddenly he put his hand around my waist and pulled me toward him. For just a minute he held me like that, our faces a little bit apart. I could feel his breath on my cheek, and smell the rum. "Come on, Annie. I could make life a lot easier for Robert and you if you got friendly with me."

I went on staring at him, feeling scared as could be. "Please let me go," I said. I started to squirm away.

He let me go and stood there looking at me. "Better think about it," he said in a harsh voice. "I can make life pretty nice for you and Robert, and I can make it pretty bad too."

"Yes, sir," I said. I made a curtsy, and then I ran out of there and headed for home.

When I got home Pa and George were out in the barnyard, sawing firewood. Ma was in the kitchen, churning butter. "Ma, he did it again."

She looked at me. "Who? What?"

"Mr. Hoggart. He came at me again. He grabbed hold of me and held me tight."

Ma banged her hand down on the top of the churn. Then she looked me in the face. "Annie, you swear it's true."

"I swear it, Ma."

She went on looking me in the face. "He grabbed you, touched you."

"He pulled me up against him, and I thought he was going to kiss me, but he didn't." I shuddered, just remembering it. "I've got to tell Pa."

She looked off at the wall, thinking. "Annie, you best leave that to me," she said finally. "Your pa's got bad money troubles."

"Troubles?"

"The price of that blamed merino ram has burst. With the price up so high people were bound to take advantage of it. Somebody brought a ship-load of them from Spain to New York. They aren't scarce anymore, and the price dropped and is still dropping, with no end in sight. Pa isn't going to get but a fraction of what he owes for his. He owes for the clock as well. People are beginning to get after him."

"He needs my wages, doesn't he, Ma?"

"Without them he's in a heap of trouble. If his creditors really want to be hard on him, he could go to prison."

I just felt sick. "So I'm stuck," I said. "He'll keep me in the mill forever and ever."

She sighed. "I hope not," she said. "I won't let him sign you on again for another six months if I can help it. But it'll be worse for all of us if he goes to debtors' prison. I'll tell him, though. I'll tell him what happened, just so he knows he'd better not sign you up again."

Chapter
NINE

THE BIG PROBLEM, that I could see right off, was that Robert and I were plain mill hands, and didn't have any right to speak to Colonel Humphreys. He was a mighty important man, and you just didn't go up to his house and knock on his door like he was an ordinary farmer. He had a big house on a hill just on the edge of Humphreysville. I knew where it was, because I'd been past it plenty of times heading down to Derby to see Ma's cousins. I could go around to the back door and tell the servants that I had a message for the colonel. But the servants weren't likely to take much note of me. They'd want to know what the message was, and all of that, and wouldn't believe me if I told them, anyway. What were we going to do? I didn't know. All I could do was go on from day to day and hope I would come up with an answer.

Two nights later, when I came home from the mill, Pa was sitting at the table waiting for me. "Sit down, Annie," he said.

I sat down at the table. "What's wrong, Pa?"

He looked at me. "Daniel Brown came by this morning. He seems to know this story of yours about Mr. Hoggart pestering you."

Daniel Brown was Hetty's pa. "I didn't tell him, Pa."

"He thought I didn't know about it. He came to warn me. It was mighty embarrassing for me, Annie."

"I swear I didn't say anything to him, Pa."

"Who did, then?"

"Hetty must have. She knows all about it."

"How does she know? Did you tell her some story?"

I blushed, for I had told her, and she'd told some of the other girls. "Pa, the girls all know. They're all afraid Mr. Hoggart will try the same on them."

"Annie, you shouldn't be spreading these stories. It could cause us a lot of trouble if it got back to Mr. Hoggart that you were spreading gossip about him."

"Pa, it's not just stories. It's true." It was making me feel sort of crazy and sick that he wouldn't believe me.

"What about that tale that Mr. Hoggart's been stealing wool? You have no proof of that."

Suddenly I was worried. Hetty had promised not to tell her pa about that. "Did Mr. Brown tell you I'd said that?"

"No," Pa said. "He didn't seem to have heard that."

So Hetty hadn't told. "It's true, anyway."

"Annie, you can't go around saying things like that without proof."

But we had proof. I'd seen that cabin in the woods. "Pa—" Then I realized that I couldn't say anything about it, for he'd be dreadful angry at me if he found out I'd tracked Mr. Hoggart through the woods. "Robert says the tally sheets didn't work out. That's proof."

"No, it's not." He slapped the palm of his hand down on the table. "It doesn't prove anything at all. There could be a whole lot behind this that you don't know anything about." He gave me a stern look. "Now, I want you to stop all this. We could get into serious trouble if it got back to Mr. Hoggart that you were spreading these kinds of rumors about him."

Well, there wasn't any point in trying to argue with him. I had a funny feeling that he believed me, at least partly. He'd known me all my life, and he knew I wasn't the kind to make up stories like that. But what with the mess he'd got himself in, he couldn't afford to believe me. For if he believed me, he'd have to take me out of the mill.

Anyway, I realized that I'd better make sure Hetty didn't tell her pa about the wool, so that night I walked her home. "Did you know your pa came to see my pa about what Mr. Hoggart tried to do to me?"

"He said he was going to. I figured maybe he could get your pa to take it serious."

"It didn't help. Pa still doesn't believe it. He told your pa it was all just stories."

"But it isn't stories," Hetty said. "The girls all know about it."

"Hetty, you didn't tell your pa about Mr. Hoggart stealing wool, did you?"

"Oh, no," she said. "You made me promise. Besides, I don't know as Pa would believe it unless you had proof."

But now I had proof. I wondered: Ought I to tell Mr. Brown myself? "Hetty, does your pa know Colonel Humphreys?"

"I think he knows him some," Hetty said. "He made a farm wagon for him once, and he mends his wagon wheels for him sometimes. I reckon he knows him."

But I decided I'd better talk it over with Robert before I said anything more. So I changed the subject, and we talked about the new bonnet Hetty was making herself until we got to her house and I headed for home.

For the next few days I hardly got a chance to see Robert. Mr. Hoggart had got him limping here and limping there all day long, carrying things. It was taking all the strength out of him, and the few times I saw him he looked so tired I didn't want to bring up anything that would cause him worry. But finally I did. "Robert, Mr. Brown knows Colonel Humphreys. Leastwise, he did some work for him."

Robert thought about it. "Annie, I reckon we ought to go slow. We still aren't exactly sure that there's wool in that cabin. Suppose we got Mr. Brown to go out there and break into the place, and there wasn't any wool? That'd be the end of you and me. Mr. Hoggart would let me go first thing. I'd have to leave town for sure then."

"But you can't go on like this, Robert. It'll kill you."

"Oh, I'll manage for a while. Meanwhile we'll keep our eyes open and see if we can get better proof."

"Well, then we have to go back out to the cabin some night and find out."

"We could try it. But we'd have to find a way to open the lock."

"I'll think of something."

It snowed some that night, and off and on the next day, and then the sky cleared and the temperature began to drop. We were in for a real cold spell, with everything frozen up tight. Pa and George took the ox sledge over to the woodlot, where last year's cutting was piled, ready to be sawed and split. They were gone all day, and when they came back the sweat was freezing to their faces. But they had enough firewood to hold us through a cold spell, if it didn't go on for more than a week or so.

Pa was still campaigning about the clock; he wouldn't let up on it. We had our meals to it, said our prayers to it, and went to bed to it. Ma fought it off as best she could. Meals didn't come just so, but ten or fifteen minutes late, and when Pa told her it was time for bed she'd generally find something that had to be done, leaving Pa to grumble—why couldn't it wait until morning, or why hadn't she thought of it before. But she couldn't stretch it too far: She knew Pa had the right and duty to set the rules around the house. He wouldn't let off talking about it. We had to hear about it all the time. "It's a marvel," Pa said. "Once only the rich could afford clocks, but with the new methods of manufacturing, these mechanisms will soon be found in every home, no matter how humble. That's the great value of these new methods. Where it used to take a clockmaker a week to make one of these, six men in a factory using this system can turn out several a day."

"Bound to put a lot of clockmakers out of work, I should reckon," Ma said.

"Not a bit of it," Pa said. "That's the beauty of the new system. It brings the price down so that every farmer in the country can afford to own a clock. Naturally, demand for clocks will shoot up, and soon there'll be more clockmakers at work than ever. You'll see."

"Well, I hope all the farmers don't go into the mills," Ma said. "Otherwise we're going to be a little short of food."

"Not a bit of it," Pa said. "It'll be the same thing in farming as in anything else. Science, new methods, everything up-to-date. There'll be machines for planting, machines for cultivating, machines for cutting wood, machines for everything. Work to the clock, instead of leaving it to nature.

Think of how much labor is lost in the winter when the days grow short. With the new methods we won't need but half the farms we have, and the farmers will be free to go into the mills. Why, it won't be long before home spinning has disappeared. With machines, the price of cloth has got so, it's hardly worth making your own at home. Someday the spinning wheel will be a relic, a reminder of the olden times. People will laugh at the idea of making your own cloth at home."

I was mighty sick of hearing about all this, and I went out to the barn to feed the chickens. It had gotten even colder than before. I'd put a pan of water out in the barn for the chickens before dinner. It was frozen solid—not just on the top, but all the way down to the bottom. I turned the pan upside down and banged it, and the ice fell out in a chunk. I filled the pan up again, but I knew it wasn't much use—it'd be frozen over pretty soon.

In the morning I bundled up real good for my walk to the mill, but the cold went right through my clothes, and I had to keep clapping at my sides with my hands to stir up some heat. My nose like to froze off. I pulled my scarf up over my nose and mouth, just leaving my eyes showing. But that wasn't any good because my breath soon soaked the scarf, and it would have frozen to my lips if I hadn't pulled it away. After that, about every two minutes I'd pull my hand out of my mitten and hold it over my nose; and about the time my nose was warmed up my hand would be stinging and I'd put it back in my mitten again.

Cold as it was, the snow was almost like ice. It was like trying to walk across a frozen pond, except that the snow wasn't flat like a pond, but rutted and twisted. About every ten steps I slipped, and I fell down twice. Oh, I was pretty miserable by the time I got to the mill; and between trying to keep my nose from freezing off, and slipping and sliding, I was late when I got there, and worried that I was going to catch it from Mr. Hoggart.

I needn't have worried, for his mind was occupied with something else. The great waterwheel that ran the machinery was icing up. As I came up the mill road I could see Mr. Hoggart and a couple of the New York boys standing by the shunt where the water ran under the wheel, trying to poke ice off it with long poles. The ice was clustering around the spokes and struts that the wheel was built of. That ice was heavy, and was slowing the wheel down a good deal. But the worst was, if the wheel iced up enough it would quit moving altogether. The machines would stop, and we wouldn't be able to card or spin or anything else until they got the wheel loose again.

Mr. Hoggart had those poor boys knocking ice off that wheel with those heavy poles all day. He'd keep two or three of them down there until they were soaked and near frozen to death, and crying from the cold. Then he'd send them inside to thaw out and push another two or three out to handle the poles. To warm them up a little he'd give each of them a swallow of rum before they went out, and another when they came back; and of course he'd take one himself along the way. He was going to be drunk before the day was out, and I knew I'd best keep out of his way.

I thought about Mr. Hoggart pestering me all afternoon, and finally decided I'd slip out and head for home a few minutes early. Mr. Hoggart wasn't thinking about anything but the waterwheel, for if it froze up and the mill stopped, Colonel Humphreys would lose a good deal of money. It was Mr. Hoggart's place to see that things like that didn't happen.

So I kept an eye on the clock in the bell tower and when it got to be just a few minutes before five, I told Hetty that I was feeling sick and thought I was going to throw up. I grabbed my coat, and went on out of the slubbing room and down the long stairs to the ground.

I stood for a moment at the bottom of the stairs, listening. Over the rumble of machinery coming from inside the building I could hear the thumps and shouts and curses of the boys whacking ice off the waterwheel. I felt sorry for them; they'd be doing that all night, so the wheel wouldn't freeze up at night.

I listened for the sound of Mr. Hoggart's voice. I didn't hear it. I wished I knew where he was, but I didn't dare look around the corner of the building to the waterwheel to see if he was there. I went around the building the other way, out to the mill road. A line of alder bushes ran alongside the mill road. I slipped in behind them on the snowy field so as to be out of sight of the mill as much as possible. Of course, the bushes were bare of leaves, but the alders were thick and covered me up pretty fair.

The snow was crusted over as hard as brick and as slippery as butter. I had to hang onto the alder bushes to keep from falling down. I went on slipping and sliding down toward the town road. And I was halfway there when I saw Mr. Hoggart turn off the town road onto the mill road. He was carrying a jug of rum, and slipping and sliding himself.

I was scared as I could be, for if he looked close he was bound to see me through the alders. I stopped moving, and crouched down, getting colder by the minute. On he came, cursing when he slipped, and carrying the jug cradled in his arms, so it would be protected if he fell down. He'd rather break an arm than that jug, I figured. He was concentrating on his footing, and keeping his eyes on the dips and ruts in the road, and I prayed that he'd keep on doing that until he got by me. He kept on coming until he was abreast of me. Then he stopped, uncorked the jug, and raised it to his lips. With the jug in midair, he looked around to see if anyone was noticing him. The only person he saw was me crouched down behind the alders.

"You," he shouted. "Where do you think you're going?" He bent over and set the jug down on the frozen snow. I didn't wait but started on out of there, slipping and sliding along behind the alders, grabbing hold of them as I went. But I was licked, because he was out on the mill road, which was chewed up, and gave him better footing than I was getting in the field of frozen snow behind the alders. He followed along abreast of me, cursing and shouting, and trying to grab me through the alder bushes. I was as scared as could be, my heart thumping, and sweating even in that cold.

"Hold still, damn you," he shouted. I didn't stop, but went on scrambling along toward the town road. I figured, if I made it safely there I could make a run for it. I might have a chance then, because he wouldn't want anybody to see him chasing a mill girl down the road.

All of a sudden he made a dive for me, into the alders. He crashed through them and fell on his belly. I turned to run out across the snowfield. I didn't make more than ten feet before I slipped and went down. He kneeled up, dove across the slick snow, and was on me. I staggered to my feet. He swatted me across the face, knocking me back onto the snow. Tears began to leak out of my eyes. Then he looked down at me. "If I didn't have that water-wheel to worry about, I'd teach you a lesson you'd never forget, miss. Now, you go on back to the mill. I'll tend to you later."

Chapter
TEN

—I WASN'T GOING BACK to the mill, that was for sure. Not the way Mr. Hoggart was then, drunk and mad and ready to do anything. But I didn't want to go home, either. What with being hit, and crying, and falling into the snow, and getting my coat ripped, I looked pretty bad. Pa and Ma would want to know what it was all about. I couldn't tell them, because they wouldn't believe me. Pa wouldn't blame Mr. Hoggart for being provoked with us, he'd say. I was exaggerating, he'd say, in order to get out of my contract, he'd say. No, it was hopeless to try to tell them anything. I had to get cleaned up before I went home, so they wouldn't ask questions.

Where could I go? I thought about the people we knew in Humphreysville—the minister, our friends. The people I knew best in the village were Hetty Brown's folks. It'd be some comfort just to be there, and I could clean up a little.

I went on down the mill road, turned onto the village road, and pretty soon I came to their place. I knocked at the door. Hetty's ma opened it. She took one look and her eyes went wide. "What on earth happened to you, Annie?"

I put my hands over my face and began to cry. Mrs. Brown sort of pulled me in, and took me over to the fire. Oh, my, that fire felt good.

"What happened, Annie?" Mrs. Brown said again.

"Mr. Hoggart was drunk. He whacked me and knocked me down. He's always pestering me, and he's trying to work Robert to death. He'll do it if he can."

She gave me a squeeze. "You just wait here and warm up." She went out to the back of the house where Mr. Brown's wheel shop was, and in a minute she came back with him.

Mr. Brown was the biggest man in the village, I'd always heard, and I could believe it. He was way over six feet tall, and his head nearly scraped the ceiling beams as he came into the room. He was so big that he seemed to fill up the room all by himself. But he was kindly; anyone could see that by the wrinkles at the corners of his eyes. He came over and sat down in a rocking chair next to me.

"Tell me about it, Annie," he said. "What's this all about?" He put his huge hand over mine.

I was ashamed of crying, but the idea of somebody willing to listen to my story did it. After a minute I quit, and wiped my face off with the sleeve of my coat. "Mr. Hoggart was drunk. He whacked me and knocked me down. He's always pestering me, and he's trying to kill Robert. He'll do it if he can."

They both became very still and looked at me, because they saw I meant it. They knew that something bad was going on. Mr. Brown put his hand on my shoulder, and bent down a little toward me. "Tell me about it, Annie. What's happening?"

So I told him the whole thing right from the beginning: How Robert had figured out Mr. Hoggart was stealing; how we'd caught him, and the cabin and all that; how Mr. Hoggart had had it in for us ever since, always pestering me, and forcing Robert to do work that was like to kill him.

They listened all the way through, with Mrs. Brown's eyes getting wider and wider, and Mr. Brown asking a little question here and there just to make sure he was getting everything right. When I finished, he said, "You see what the problem is, don't you, Annie? It's his word against yours."

"We have proof, sir," I said. "There's that cabin. And we saw him filling that sack."

"How did you happen to come upon him doing that?"

"I went up there to ask him not to dock me for being late once. Robert went with me. We saw him with a big sack he was loading with wool."

Mr. Brown shook his head. "That doesn't mean very much. He could have had a dozen reasons for filling a sack with wool. Besides, he'll just deny it."

I could see that was true. "Mr. Brown, I have

to get out of that mill. He's pestering me all the time."

He thought for a minute. "Did he actually touch you?"

"He tried to grab me."

Mr. Brown frowned. "Are you sure of that, Annie? Are you sure he wasn't just teasing you?"

"Sir, he *did* grab me."

He didn't say anything, but sat looking at me for a moment. "These are hard accusations, Annie."

"It's true, sir. He tried to do worse than that last Wednesday after work, but some of the girls figured what he was up to, and sent Robert."

"Robert saw this—incident?"

"Yes, sir. He did, sir."

He sat there, frowning and thinking. Finally he said, "Annie, you didn't do anything to encourage this—behavior, did you? Mr. Hoggart's in a position to do nice things for the mill girls. Give them easy jobs and such. I suppose it might occur to some girls that it would be worth playing up to Mr. Hoggart a little."

I nodded. "He said if I was nice to him he'd make things easy for me and Robert, and if I wasn't he'd make things hard. But I wouldn't do it. I'd never do it. I hate him."

"Shhh, Annie. You mustn't say things like that. Mr. Hoggart is well regarded here. He's done a good job with the woolen mill."

I looked down at the floor. It sounded like he

wasn't going to believe me. What would I do then? "I'm sorry," I said.

"You know, Annie, I can't just go on your word about all of this. I need proof, I need evidence. If Mr. Hoggart's been stealing, of course I'll go to Colonel Humphreys. But I can't go with just your word."

"But we found the cabin, sir. That's the proof. The wool's in the cabin."

"Did you actually see this cabin? Did you go inside? Or did you see Mr. Hoggart bringing wool there?"

I was stuck. For a minute I thought of lying and saying that I'd been inside the cabin. But I didn't dare.

"Well, I didn't actually get inside the cabin, for Mr. Hoggart was in there. But I heard noises in there, and I saw him after he came out."

"How did that come about?" Mr. Brown said. "There are too many mysteries here, Annie."

I took a deep breath. "One Sunday night when I was coming here I saw footprints leading from the mill out to the woods. So I took a chance and followed them, and heard him in there."

Mr. Brown shook his head. "So you don't really know whether he's actually storing wool in that shed or not. He could have been out there for a perfectly good reason."

"There has to be wool in there, sir. What else could it be?"

"I admit, Annie, it looks that way. But it isn't

proof. I know you, and I know you wouldn't make a thing like this up. I'm willing to admit you and Robert might be right about it. But mill hands are always talking against overseers, and Colonel Humphreys won't take it seriously unless there's something monstrous wrong. Let's admit that Mr. Hoggart is doing a little pilfering. A lot of overseers do it. But it doesn't usually amount to very much. Oh, they'll siphon off a bottle of rum, or take some lumber and nails out of the storeroom to make a table with, or bring home some yarn for their wives. Most of the owners accept this kind of petty thievery as part of the game. If they've got a good overseer, as Mr. Hoggart appears to be, they'll wink at it. I'm not saying you're a liar. So if you tell me you saw Mr. Hoggart taking some wool out of the mill, I'll accept that. But you know, Annie, my guess is that Colonel Humphreys wouldn't care even if you had a dozen witnesses. He'd rather let it go, and keep Mr. Hoggart content, than make a fuss over a small matter and lose a good overseer."

But it wasn't just petty pilfering. "Sir—"

He held up his hand to stop me. "Now, as far as this business of his pestering you, forcing his attentions on you—well, you're a pretty girl. These things happen. I expect he'd been drinking."

"Yes, sir."

"We all know he has a weakness for rum. But so long as it doesn't interfere with the work, I don't imagine that Colonel Humphreys wants to know about that, either."

I was feeling mighty low. All along I'd figured that if I told somebody I'd have a chance. But it didn't look that way. "Mr. Brown, I just have to get out of the mill."

"The best advice I can give you is to stay out of his way as much as possible. When's your contract up?"

"In April, sir."

"That's less than three months. If you're still unhappy at the mill, I don't suppose your pa would want you to stay on beyond that."

There was nothing more for me to say. I stood up. "Well, thank you, sir, for all the trouble I put you to."

I cleaned myself up, for I didn't want Pa and Ma to know anything about it, especially that I'd told Mr. Brown the whole story.

Pa was too busy watching the clock to see how late I was, to notice that I was scuffed up a little, and when Ma did notice the bruise on my face I said I'd slipped on the ice on the road and fell, and had gone to the Browns' to clean up, which was why I was late.

I went off to the mill the next morning feeling dreadful low. It seemed like there was no escape. I'd have to last out the next three months until my contract was up, and pray that Pa wouldn't sign me up again. Oh, I was trapped, and there wasn't any way out.

On top of it, it was still mighty cold. I kept flapping my arms and trying to keep my nose from freezing. It made me late again, and when I was a half mile away I began to run, slipping and sliding on the icy snow. I was concentrating so hard on trying not to fall down that I was actually going into the mill before I realized that something was wrong. The place was dead quiet; none of the machines were running.

I raced upstairs to my slubbing billy, to get there before Mr. Hoggart missed me. But I didn't have to worry. The girls were all away from the machines, standing at the windows, looking downward.

"What happened?"

"The waterwheel's frozen solid with ice. It won't turn until they can knock the ice off."

I leaned out the window to look for myself. I was almost directly above the wheel, and had a good view of what was going on. There was ice all over the banks of the shunt and a coating of ice on top of the water in the shunt, although the water beneath was still flowing through the shunt, down the spillway, and under the waterwheel. But the wheel was not turning; it was standing still. There was ice all over it—on the spokes, on the blades, and down between the wheel itself and the walls of the spillway. Mr. Hoggart was down there, with three boys who were jabbing at the ice with poles. He was cursing a lot, for every minute that wheel stood idle it cost Colonel Humphreys money.

They weren't having much luck. The ice was hard and thick and wouldn't crack easily. It was

pretty plain that poles weren't going to do it; they'd need to hack that ice out with axes. Not that we girls were in any blame hurry to see that wheel moving again. It was like a holiday for us. Every time one of the boys took a whack at the ice and nothing happened, we'd let out a low cheer. The other boys were hanging out the windows, the same as us. They were jeering and shouting at the boys down below, crying out, "Why, you ain't got the strength of a fly, nor the brains either," and roaring with laughter when one of the boys down below slipped on the ice and fell, even though they knew that soon enough they'd have to take their turns with the poles.

Then Mr. Hoggart said something to one of the boys. The boy dropped his pole and trotted off out of sight around the corner of the building. The other boys stood there, leaning on the poles, and the boys leaning out the windows began to jeer even louder, until Mr. Hoggart shook a fist at them and cursed, and they shut up for a little.

We waited, and in a couple of minutes the boy came back into sight, carrying an ax. He went over to the waterwheel, and began to hack at the ice. The main trouble was the ice that was frozen between the wheel and the wall of the spillway it turned in. If they could clear the ice out from there, and from the same place on the other side of the wheel, up against the mill, the wheel would move again.

The boys went on hacking. The ice was spraying up into the sunlight, sparkling yellow as gold. It was a pretty sight. We girls went on leaning out the windows, watching. They'd get the wheel moving in time, but in the meanwhile we could enjoy our holiday.

After a while the boy with the ax got tired, and another one took his place. Mr. Hoggart said something to the boy who had just quit. Off he went out of sight around the corner of the building. In about two minutes he was back. Coming along behind him was Robert. He was having a lot of trouble keeping his footing on the ice around the spillway.

Mr. Hoggart picked up one of the poles and jammed it down between the wheel and the wall of the spillway. It went pretty far down, which meant that they'd got that side of the wheel pretty well cleared. Mr. Hoggart stood back, the boy went to work again with the ax, and in a moment that side of the wheel was free.

Now Mr. Hoggart turned to Robert and said something. Robert took the ax and limped to the wheel. But he did not lean down and start hacking at the ice. Instead, he began to climb up on the wheel, holding onto the icy struts with one hand, carrying the ax with the other. It was going to be his job to hack the ice out from between the wheel and the other side of the spillway.

The problem was that to do that he'd have to work from on top of the waterwheel itself. The wheel was right up against the side of the mill.

There wasn't any place to get at the ice, except from up on the wheel.

Now he was lying on top of the wheel, facedown. He began swinging the ax into the space between the wheel and the mill wall. Suddenly my back went all chill and my heart began to race. For I saw what it was all about. Once Robert had chopped a certain amount of ice out, the pressure of the water would suddenly break the wheel free. There was no telling in advance when that moment would come. The wheel would suddenly begin to turn, and where would Robert be then? If he had two good feet, he could quickly stand and make a jump for it. But with that bad foot Robert wasn't much for standing quickly, much less jumping. One little slip and he'd be gone over the wheel into the spillway, with that wheel turning on top of him.

I grabbed up my coat and raced out of the slubbing room, down the long flight of stairs and around the back of the mill, where Mr. Hoggart couldn't see me. I ran on, slipping and sliding down the mill road, until I got to the village road. Here the footing was better. I went on running, my feet twisting and turning in the ruts, until I got to the Browns'. I banged on the door, and then waited. In a minute the door swung open, and there was Mrs. Brown. "Annie—"

"Mr. Brown's got to come right away," I shouted. "Mr. Hoggart's put Robert on top of the waterwheel to chop out the ice. He's trying to kill Robert. He's bound to be flung into the spillway when the wheel breaks free. He can't jump like the rest."

"Lord, is this true, Annie?" She turned away from the door, and in a minute Mr. Brown was there.

"What's this, Annie?"

"He's trying to kill Robert. I know he is." I stood there, my heart pounding.

Mr. Brown stood there for a minute, thinking. Then he said, "It doesn't sound right putting a boy with that lame foot up on the wheel. I'd better go have a look."

"Please, sir, hurry."

He grabbed his coat, and began to run out of the house, putting his coat on as he went. I came running on behind him, but he was going a good deal faster than I could go. He reached the mill road when I was still a good piece away. I saw him turn up the mill road, stagger on a patch of ice, straighten up, and go on up the road. In a minute he disappeared around the side of the mill. I went on running. I turned into the mill road and began to work my way up it as quick as I could. I reached the mill, and started for the side when Mr. Brown suddenly appeared.

He stood in front of me, barring my way. I stopped. Then he put his arm around my shoulder and gently turned me around. "Better not go back there, Annie," he said. "You don't want to see it."

I screamed, broke away from him, and dashed around the corner toward the waterwheel. Two boys were coming toward me, carrying something heavy. I screamed again, and then they came by me.

Robert's body was soaked in water, and already the ice was forming on his face, his eyes, his clothes. His nose was squashed down and one eye was just a pool of blood. His other pale blue eye was open and just stared out. His clothes were torn, and his body was limp as an empty sack, for most of his bones had been broken by the wheel. The one thing I never forgot was his foot. It was bare, and twisted all the way around so that it was pointed backward. I screamed, and then Mr. Brown picked me up and carried me away.

Chapter
ELEVEN

THERE WAS PLENTY OF TALK in the village about it. A lot of people said that Mr. Hoggart was in the wrong of it, and thought he ought to be dismissed before he hurt somebody else. A lot of other people said he wasn't to blame; it was an accident. The boys had all been taking turns and it was just Robert's hard luck that he was the one on the wheel when it started to move. Besides, it wasn't Mr. Hoggart's fault that Robert hadn't been able to jump off quick enough.

Robert's pa went to the justice of the peace and talked about bringing charges against Mr. Hoggart. The justice of the peace told him there wasn't anything to be done about it. It was an accident. There were always accidents in mills, everybody knew that; and if you went to work in a mill you had to watch out for yourself. Just as there were always accidents on farms too. If Robert hadn't got his foot hurt in a farm accident, he wouldn't have been in the mill in the first place.

Pa and Ma felt just dreadful about it. They

were good friends of the Bronsons, and it hurt them
something awful to see how stricken the Bronsons
were. "Poor Robert," Pa said. "He never had a bit of
luck. First his foot, and now this."

"It wasn't any accident, Pa," I cried. "Mr. Hoggart did it on purpose."

"Now, Annie. I know how you felt about
Robert, but we can't blame Mr. Hoggart for this."

Even Ma agreed. "I don't like Mr. Hoggart,
and I don't trust him, Annie. But I can't believe he'd
do this to Robert deliberately."

The tears began to leak out of my eyes. "He
did. Yes, he did."

Ma put her arms around me. "Poor Annie. It's
been hard for you."

"It's God's will," Pa said. "There's always death
in life, and the dead must bury the dead. In time,
we'll be reconciled to it."

But then George spoke up. "I believe Annie,"
he said quietly. "I believe Hoggart did it on purpose."

We all looked at him. "What makes you think
that, George?" Ma said.

He didn't say anything for a minute. Then he
said, "I just have a feeling about it. I don't like the
man. I never did. Since this happened I met a man
from where Hoggart worked before he came here.
The rumor's true—Hoggart lost his position there
because he was pestering the girls."

Pa stared at George. "Who told you that?"

"One of the men who works at the Derby saw-
mill. He says everybody knows it."

"Rumors," Pa said. "Just rumors."

"I don't think so," George said. "Pa, if it was
me, I'd take Annie out of the mill."

"George, it's your father's business," Ma said.

"That may be so," George said. "But if it was
me, I wouldn't have her in the mill." He stood up.
"I'm going to see to the ox." He didn't say anything
more, but went out through the back door, and into
the night. I sat there for a minute, wiping my eyes,
and trying to get a hold on myself. Then I stood up.
"I'll go collect the eggs." And I went out after
George.

He was pouring a bucket of water in the ox's
trough. "George," I said. "Why did you say that?"

He shook his head. "I don't know why I both-
ered. There's nothing Pa can do. He's near ruined
with debt, and he's depending on your wages to
keep him going. I think down inside he knows he
ought to take you out of the mill. But he can't allow
himself to believe that, for he'll be in serious trouble
if he lets you stay home."

"Why can't he just give that blame clock
back?"

George shrugged. "That's Pa's stubbornness. If
he gives the clock back it's like admitting he failed.
He can't admit that, even to himself."

I looked at George. "What am I going to do?"

"If it happens again, don't bother Pa about it.
You tell me." It made me feel better to hear him say

that. But nothing could make me feel much better, because of Robert.

The worst of it was to go on working at the mill. Robert's burial was that Sunday, and Pa let me stay home until then. But on the next Monday I had to go back to the mill. Pa had signed the contract. I didn't have any choice. But it had less than three months to go. I had to get through that.

It was just dreadful. I had to stand there all day long, with that waterwheel turning around and around below me, trying not to think of Robert being caught under it and his bones all smashed. I hoped it hadn't hurt him much. I hoped it had killed him quick, before it started to break up his bones. Those first days back at the mill I thought a lot about jumping out the window on top of the water-wheel myself.

After a few days I knew I couldn't go on like that. I just couldn't stand the pain. I knew I had to put Robert out of my mind, or die myself. The trouble was that I had too much time to think. So, when I was standing at my slubbing billy or walking back and forth to the mill, I tried to go over the eight-times table in my head, or work out what countries were next to France. Finally, after another week or so, there came times when I wouldn't think about Robert for a whole hour at a stretch. But then something would happen that would remind me of him—I'd hear somebody use an expression he liked, or a song he used to sing, and it would all come up again. Of course, I had to walk past his house every morning and every night; and there was always that awful waterwheel.

The one good thing that came out of it was that Mr. Hoggart stayed away from me. He knew that there was talk against him in the village, and he didn't want to add to it. But I figured he still had a grudge against me, and when he thought the talk over Robert had died down, he'd try to get even.

Just to look at Mr. Hoggart, knowing that he'd killed Robert, made me feel sick and tremble. Oh, I hated him, I hated that waterwheel, I hated that mill. I had to get out of there. I'd stick it out until spring; I figured I could get through that. Then if Pa signed me on again—well, I didn't know what I'd do. I'd run away. I'd go down to New Haven, or New York, or even out west. But I wasn't going to stay in that mill. I'd kill myself first. I'd jump down on that waterwheel and let it grind me up the way it ground up Robert.

Running away wouldn't be easy, not for a girl anyway. Even grown women didn't travel on their own unless they were obliged to for some particular reason, and then they'd go by coach. Nobody thought twice of seeing a strange boy walking along a road, for they'd figure he was carrying a message or was sent by his pa or his master to fetch something. But anyone who saw a strange girl going along by herself would think it was dreadful odd, and would get to asking a lot of questions.

I'd have to dress up like a boy. I'd heard stories about women doing that. There was one woman who became a sailor and went to sea for years until her ship was wrecked off Montauk, and when her body drifted in and they went to bury it, they found out she was a woman. I'd heard a lot of stories like that, so I knew that I could probably disguise myself as a boy all right. But where would I get boys' clothes? Oh, there would be a lot of problems to it. The truth is, I didn't want to run away. I was sure to be homesick in a strange place among strangers. I'd miss Ma something awful, and Pa, too, when you got down to it. I'd miss our house and our fields and even that blame merino ram. Oh, I wasn't going to run away if there was a way around it. But if I had to stay in the mill, I would.

Visiting the Browns' helped to take my mind off Robert. Hetty knew how I was feeling and chattered away about her bonnet and how many different colors of ribbon you could buy at the store, and such things. Talking to her cheered me up a little, and I went by there pretty frequently, and sometimes, if the weather was bad, I'd stay for the night. For a change Pa didn't bother me about being late getting home sometimes. He knew how I was feeling.

So the weeks went by, and the end of my contract came closer. I kept counting the days, and visiting Hetty from time to time. One night I was coming home after seeing her, watching the moon rise over the snowy fields, making the evening near as bright as day, feeling sad and lonely and wishing time would speed up so I could get out of the mill.

I came to our farm lane, and turned in; and as I did I saw up ahead a creature so strange I came to a dead stop. It was bumping along slow in the bright moonlight, looking like a bear with horns, or a calf up on its hind legs. I shivered, and started to run; and the creature stopped, and sort of shifted around, and I saw that it was not an animal, but a human—a man carrying something on his back. He stood still a minute to shift his load, and I came up closer. I could make out a man with a saddle slung across his shoulders, and on top of the saddle were hung a pot and a long-handled skillet and some other things I couldn't make out. But as I came up right next to him, I saw it was Pa, and I knew right away what he'd done. He'd bought the saddle. And I knew the only way he could have bought it was to sign me on at the mill for another six months.

"Pa, you didn't. Pa, you wouldn't do that to me."

"Annie, I don't want to hear anything about it. It's done. Besides, I think you've got Mr. Hoggart all wrong. He told me you were a good worker and he wants to keep you on. He said that if you were obedient and did what you were told, he might improve your position in time. Instead of working at the slubbing billy, he'd put you in charge of filling the lamps, cleaning them when they needed it, lighting them when it got dark. He said it was a much easier job, all the girls wanted it, but he'd give it to you if you behaved well."

"Pa," I cried. "Don't you see what he means by that?"

"Now, Annie, you've let your imagination run away with you. Perhaps there was an incident of some sort. I know that Mr. Hoggart has a weakness for drink, and I can allow that he said something he shouldn't have when he was drinking. But you shouldn't exaggerate."

"Pa, I'm not exaggerating," I shouted. "I'm not exaggerating."

"Now, you listen to me, my girl," he said, raising his voice. "I won't have you shouting at me. I've made my decision about this, and it's final. Everybody has a job to do in this world. Why should you think you're an exception?"

I tried to keep my voice down. "I don't mind working, Pa. But not in the mill. Not after what happened to Robert. I think about him all the time and it's making me crazy."

Pa looked off away from me. "Annie, nobody's sure about that. It seems like Robert was just taking his turn along with the rest of them."

"No," I shouted. He reached back his hand to smack me. "I'm sorry," I said. "I didn't mean to shout."

He frowned at me. "Annie, since Robert died we've been mighty easy on you. Don't start taking advantage of it."

I didn't say anything. Then I said, "How long is it for?"

He couldn't look at me. He turned his eyes down to the ground, and then so as not to show weakness looked off at the moon again. "Only another six months. After that, if you still don't like it, I won't make you stay in the mill anymore."

Our eyes met. It was almost like he was begging me to forgive him. But I couldn't. I hated him for what he'd done.

He turned, and with that saddle on his back and all those things in the saddle clanking like cowbells, he headed for the house. I stood there watching him go, hating him, hating Mr. Hoggart, hating the mill, hating Humphreysville. What was to become of me now? He'd go on signing me up at the mill year after year, using my wages to buy the things he had to have. Oh, I knew he couldn't help himself; once he got his mind set on having something, he couldn't rest until he'd got it. It wasn't any use trying to stop him. Ma had found that out a long time ago. And so I was stuck. There wouldn't be any way out, and I'd go on working at the mill for years and years, so desperate to get out I'd be willing to marry the first one who asked me.

And what was I getting for all my trouble? I'd come to be everybody's toy, for them to play with as they liked: Pa's toy and Mr. Hoggart's toy, and Colonel Humphreys' toy, when you got down to it. They all had something they wanted from me, and they were determined to get what they wanted. Me,

I just didn't come into it, any way I could see. They'd got their minds made up as to what I must do, and what I should be, and that was the end of it. Nobody cared what I wanted; that was clear as day. All they were interested in was what they wanted from me.

Oh, I hated them all. And standing there in the moonlight, I knew I was going to run away. They hadn't given me any choice. But before I did, I was going to get the proof that Mr. Hoggart was stealing wool.

I would do anything to get even with him.

Chapter
TWELVE

SO THERE IT WAS. Oh, it was as scary as could be. I wished I'd had someone to talk it over with. Sometimes I talked to Robert about it in my head, like he was still alive. I could hear his voice saying that running away would be mighty rough and risky. Then I would realize that Robert was dead and wasn't saying anything at all and I'd start to cry. After a while I decided not to talk to Robert anymore. Running away from your family was hard, but I had to.

So that was my plan. It scared me a good deal. For one thing, going off by myself, with nobody for company, was dreadful worrisome. Who would be there to help me if I fell sick? Who'd be there to brace me up when I felt lonely?

I knew I'd have to be smart about it. A lot of people would be after me. Pa and Ma would want me back, because I was their daughter, and they'd miss me. And of course Pa needed my salary to clear up his debts. Mr. Hoggart would want me back because he had a contract for six months' work. The justices of the peace would want me back, because girls weren't supposed to run away.

How would I do it? Where would I go? It wouldn't be safe for a girl to travel by herself any distance, into places where she wasn't known.

Where was I going to get a suit of boy's clothes? Actually, all I needed was a pair of trousers and a hat. That'd be enough. But where was I to get trousers?

What about Tom Thrush? I wondered: Did he have any extra clothes? I figured he must have at least one extra pair of trousers. The boys were supposed to wash themselves and their clothes now and again. Colonel Humphreys had some kind of rule about that, so as to keep down the diseases and lice. I figured they each had to have at least one extra suit of clothes to wear while the main one was being washed.

I waited for my chance, and in a couple of days I cornered Tom at five o'clock after work. We waited there in the slubbing room until the others had all gone. Then I said, "Tom, can you keep a secret?"

"Yes, Miss Annie. I won't tell nobody." He squinted at me. "You couldn't get it out of me with knives."

I wasn't so sure of that. I'd heard Tom squeal pretty loud when Mr. Hoggart walloped him. He wasn't one for thinking things through before he spoke, and was always likely to let something slip. But I had to chance it. "You promise, Tom."

"I swear to it. If I swear to anything, it's certain."

"I'm going to run away."

His eyes got wide. "You mean it?"

"Yes."

"You wouldn't be scairt?"

"No. Well, a little. But I'm going to do it."

He squinted at me for a minute, thinking—or whatever you would call it, in his case. Then he said, "I'll go with you, Miss Annie. We'll run off together."

Well, I'd never thought of that, and it gave me a funny feeling. You couldn't trust Tom as far as you could throw him. He lied all the time, and stole anything he could, and he was likely to get us in trouble. But when the idea sunk in a little, I could see that it might have some advantages. Tom knew how to get around things. He'd spent most of his life looking after himself, and he knew a dreadful lot I didn't know. Besides, he'd be company. But I decided to be cautious. "I don't know, Tom. I wouldn't want to get you in trouble."

"There never was a time when I wasn't in trouble, Miss Annie. I'm used to it. I wouldn't feel comfortable if I wasn't in trouble. It wouldn't be natural to me."

"Well, maybe," I said.

"Where was you figurin' on runnin' away to?"

"I don't know," I said. "Maybe to New Haven. Maybe down to New York. Do you think we could find work if we went to New York?"

"What on earth would you want to work for, Miss Annie? There's more things lying around the docks than you could ever make off with. There ain't no point in working."

I decided not to argue about that. But I could see that it might be a good idea to run away to New York, if Tom was to come along. He knew all about the place, and we wouldn't go hungry. "Tom, I can't go dressed as a girl. I've got to get some boys' clothes. Trousers and a hat would be enough. Can you lend me some?"

"Could if I was to go naked myself," he said.

"You've only got one suit of clothes? Just the ones you have on?"

"What's the sense of having more? You can't wear but one pair of trousers and one shirt, can you?"

"What do you do when you wash them?"

"Wash them? Why, go naked until they dry."

"Don't you freeze?" I said.

"Freeze? Who'd be fool enough to wash their clothes in the winter? You'd like to take your death."

I decided not to argue with him about that. "Do you know any way to get at least some trousers?"

He gave me a wink. "Don't you worry none about that, Miss Annie. I'll get you some trousers."

He'd steal them, that was clear. I didn't like the idea of that very much, but I couldn't see any way around it. So we shook hands on it.

We'd have to wait until warm weather came and the ground began to dry up—probably late April or May. That was a good six weeks off. I hated staying in the mill a minute more, much less a whole six weeks. But I wasn't going to leave until I'd found out about that wool Mr. Hoggart was stealing. I was going to find out about that if I died for it.

The first thing I had to do was get into that shed in the woods. I had to find out if Mr. Hoggart really was storing wool in it. For once I knew that, I'd be a step along the way to getting him in real trouble. But how was I to get in? The lock on the door was mighty big and strong. There wasn't any way I could break it off.

Was there some way to steal the key from Mr. Hoggart? That didn't seem likely. I didn't even know where he kept his keys, but I figured he didn't leave them lying around the mill where anybody could find them. He'd have them tied to his belt, or hidden somewhere. So that didn't seem likely.

What about chopping a hole in the back of the cabin? That was possible. I'd chopped enough kindling wood to know how to do it. It wouldn't take more than five minutes to bust a hole big enough to slide through.

But, of course, there wouldn't be any way to cover the hole up afterward. Next time Mr. Hoggart went out there he'd know somebody had found him out, and he'd get the wool out of there mighty quick. Besides, it was risky. You'd make a lot of noise busting a hole in the cabin with an ax. The sound of an ax carried a long way on a still day, even through the woods. Mr. Hoggart might well hear it, and come running.

Was there any way to pry the cabin up a little so you could peek under the wall? Well, I'd seen men lift up cabins before, and carry them off to a new spot. But it took a fair bunch of them and a few oxen to do it. It didn't seem likely I could do it all alone.

And then it came to me; you could dig a little tunnel underneath one of the walls. It didn't have to be much of a tunnel. All you would have to do was scoop out enough dirt so you could slide through, like a dog under a fence. And if you were small it wouldn't be much trouble at all. Who did I know who was small? Tom Thrush, that's who. Once I figured out what I was going to do, and how to do it, I felt a little better.

It took me two or three days to get a chance to talk to Tom Thrush again, but he finally came up to sweep around the machines—they had to keep the floors clean, for there was the danger of all that greasy wool catching fire. Because the machinery was banging and clanging, I was able to give him a wink, and then whisper to him to meet me up at the end of the mill road, where it turned into the village road. There were trees along there and we could talk without anybody seeing us.

So, when the five o'clock bell rang I put on my cloak, went on up the mill road, and ducked down inside a cluster of pine trees that grew there. I stood there waiting and by and by Tom came up the mill road, and slipped in among the pines with me. "I hope it ain't some foolishness, Miss Annie," he said. "It's mighty cold to be standing around in the snow for nothin'."

"It's not foolishness," I said. "I've found out a way to get Mr. Hoggart."

He gave a suspicious look. "Have you now," he said.

"I figured out a way to get into that cabin where he's got the wool."

"That a fact?" he said. He looked upward at the patches of sky you could see around the tops of the pines. "I don't expect I'm goin' to be lucky enough to be left out of it?"

"No," I said. "You're the most important one."

He went on looking at the sky. "To be honest, Miss Annie, I shouldn't mind at all if somebody else had the honor. I don't mind takin' a backseat at all. Fact is, I'd ruther."

"Don't be such a coward," I said. "You haven't even heard what it is. There isn't any risk to it at all. We're just going to dig a little trench under the hut, and you could slide in and have a look around."

"Yes, I can see where there's no risk in that. Not a bit of risk. Why, if Mr. Hoggart chanced to come by just at that moment, we'd just explain that we was out in the woods a-gatherin' nuts. He'd be bound to swallow that, seein' as most nearly every-body gathers nuts in March in the middle of the night when it's pitch dark. He'd be certain to swallow that."

"Don't be silly, Tom. Mr. Hoggart isn't going to go out there late at night."

He stopped looking at the top of the pines and the sky and looked at me. "Well, I tell you, Miss Annie. I'd like to get him, all right. You can believe that. But it ain't worth gettin' half kilt for, and maybe the other half as well."

"I thought you New York boys were always doing risky things. I'm willing to take the chance, and I'm just a girl. You wouldn't want anybody to think you were more scared than a girl, would you?"

"I've heard of worse things," he said. "Like bein' half kilt."

"Tom, you've got to do it. It's our chance to get him."

He looked down at the ground, and then up at the pine tops again, and then down at the ground some more. "Just how do you figure this ought to work, then?"

"Here's what we'll do. One night after supper I'll sneak a shovel and a pick out of our barn and come up to the mill. Then after everybody's in bed you'll sneak out. We'll go on out to that cabin, and dig a little trench under the back wall. It doesn't need to be more than six or eight inches deep, and a foot wide—maybe a little wider. It wouldn't take us half an hour to dig that trench. Then you slip inside, I hand you in an oil lamp, you get a look at what's in there, and then we scoot on out of there. There won't be anything to it."

He licked his lips. "Yes, I can see that there ain't anything to it. Any fool can dig a trench in frozen dirt in the pitch dark. Especially when you have a lot of nice warm snow to tramp around on while yer doin' it."

I reached out and shook his hand. "I knew I could count on you, Tom," I said. "Don't forget to bring an oil lamp."

He'd do it. He didn't want to, but he would. So that was set. When was I to do it? There wasn't any point in waiting, just so long as we didn't have bad weather. I waited a couple of days and then I told Tom we would do it that night. All he had to do was meet me at ten o'clock by the back of the mill, in the shadows, where nobody could see us from the boys' lodging house, or the other mill.

The one thing about that blame clock was that I could count on Ma and Pa and George going to bed at eight. I slipped on up to the loft then, too, and lay there in the dark, staring at the ceiling and feeling scared. It wasn't safe, no matter what I'd told Tom. A thousand things could go wrong.

But I was determined to do it. I was determined to get even with Mr. Hoggart for what he'd done to Robert, and determined to get out of the mill and see if I couldn't make a life for myself that suited me more than the one Pa had planned for me.

Finally, when I figured Pa and Ma and George were asleep, I slipped out of bed, climbed down the ladder from the loft, and stood for a minute in the parlor, listening. There was no sound; they were asleep. There was enough light from the coals of the fire so I could see the clock. It was after nine. I slipped out of the house, back to the barn. The chickens clucked at me softly. "Shush," I whispered. I collected a shovel and a pick, and carrying one over each shoulder so they wouldn't clink together, I went on down our lane as quick as I could. Then I walked to the mill, keeping close to the trees along the road, so as to be in the shadows. In twenty minutes I was down behind the back of the mill. I waited in the shadows, looking out at the snowy field and the woods beyond. The sky was filled with patches of clouds racing for dear life from west to east, so that at one moment the moon was shining bright upon the snowy field and the woods behind the mill, and the next moment it blinked out, so that the snow was dark gray and the woods just a blotch of black at the end of the view.

By and by I heard a sound behind me. I jumped around. It was Tom, creeping along the side of the mill in the shadows, carrying an oil lamp. "Tom," I whispered. "Why'd you come that way?"

"I didn't prize crossin' that field any more than I had to. I come around behind the mill."

He came up beside me. "We're going to have to cross that field sooner or later," I said.

He looked up at the sky, and so did I. "We'd

best wait until the moon is covered," I said, "and then make a run for it. What do you think?"

"If you want to know what I think, why, it'd be to get back into our beds as quick as possible."

"Come on, Tom. If we make a run for it when the moon's covered, it'll be safe as church. Here, you take the shovel, I'll carry the pick."

"As safe as church if it was filled with lions and on fire," he said. But he took the shovel. We stood by the corner of the mill in the dark and waited. A couple of small clouds came and went over the moon, but we could see that they wouldn't last long enough to cover us while we crossed the open field of snow. We waited some more, and then there came a long cloud, miles long, I judged. Its edge touched the moon, and the moon dimmed. "Come on, Tom," I said. I broke out of the shadow of the mill and began to run across the field, and in a moment I heard Tom running along behind me. He was scared, all right; but he was more scared of being left alone in the dark by the mill. To tell the truth, I was mighty scared myself. It was a lot darker when the moon was covered, but it wasn't anywhere near pitch dark. Anyone standing in the mill or up in the boys' lodging house who happened to look out would see us running across that field. They wouldn't be able to tell who it was; they might even think it was animals—deer, or sheep, maybe. But they'd see us, all right.

We went on running. My breath was beginning to come rough in my throat. We ran on, and in a minute we came to the edge of the woods, and plunged in. We stopped to catch our breath, and looked back across the field. Up in the boys' lodging house a little light was moving slowly from window to window across the length of the building. "What's that, Tom?"

"The watchman. He goes around sometimes just to check on the boys."

"Won't he see you're not there?"

"No," Tom said. "The boys sleep three and four to a bed, jumbled up like puppies. You couldn't tell one from the other."

"He might count them."

"Not him," Tom said. "He couldn't count over ten. Once he runs out of fingers he's stuck. Why, I can count higher than he can. I counted near up to one hundred once, and would have got there, too, but I couldn't remember what come after thirty-nine."

The light came to the end of the lodging house and disappeared. "Let's find the cabin," I said. We turned, and began to make our way through the woods. It was a good deal darker among the trees. When the moon was uncovered, a fair amount of light shone down through the branches, and we could make the trunks and branches out against the snow. But when a cloud passed over, it got so dark that we couldn't see anything unless we were right on top of it. We had to grope forward with our hands.

Going along this way, we were bound to get

off the track, and we must have circled past that cabin twice before we spotted it. But finally, when the moonlight suddenly came clear, we saw it off to our right, a black chunk in the trees. We scooted for it, and in a minute we were crouched down beside it.

The first thing we did was to check the door to see if by chance it was unlocked. We lit the lamp, and held it up so we could see. The flame fluttered in the breeze, making the shadows jump and leap. The door was locked tight. We would have to dig.

We slipped around to the back wall. We could have dug under the front wall by the door just as well, or the side walls too. But I figured Mr. Hoggart was a lot less likely to go around behind the cabin next time he came out, and wouldn't notice any loose dirt.

We set to work. Tom swung the pick, breaking the frozen earth loose, and then I shoveled it off to one side, being careful to keep it in a neat pile so I could shovel it all back in place when we were done. It was hard work, especially for Tom, who had to hold the pick handle in his good hand and sort of guide it with the stump. After a bit we began to sweat, even in the cold. Every few minutes we stopped and listened, just to make sure nobody was coming through the woods. Once we heard a loud scuffling right near to us, and we jumped. But it was only an owl fluttering through the woods after his supper.

Finally, we got enough of a trench scooped out behind the cabin for Tom to lie in. Then we began to work on the dirt floor to the cabin. This was the hard part, for Tom had to swing the pick sideways to poke it under the bottom of the wall, and then I had to scoop the dirt out from the inside. We were mighty sweaty by this time, and I knew I'd have to dry myself off later, if I wasn't to shiver all night when I was trying to sleep.

After a while we finally got enough of a trench dug. Tom lay down in it on his stomach, head first, and wiggled and squiggled his way forward. His head went under the wall, and then his back, and finally only his legs, kicking like a frog's legs, were sticking out. Then they disappeared.

I lit the oil lamp, and crouched down by the trench. The light flickered. "Tom, here's the lamp," I whispered. "Don't set the place afire." I reached the lamp under the wall, and then I felt Tom's hand, and he took the lamp.

For a minute there was silence, and I waited. Finally I said, "Tom, what's in there?"

"Wool. Bags of it."

"How many bags?"

"Oh, heaps of them."

I wished I knew exactly, for it was better evidence if you could say you counted twelve or eighteen or whatever it was. But there wasn't any point in asking Tom, for he couldn't count beyond ten, no matter what he said. "Come on out, Tom."

So he blew out the lamp and shoved it out, and then scrambled out himself. I lay down in the trench and smoothed the dirt inside as best as I could. Then

I caught hold of a corner of the bottom of the wool bag, and pulled it over the loose dirt, so it wouldn't show. I slid out of the trench. We shoveled the dirt back into it, and then covered it over with snow. After that we scuffed up our footprints so that it would look like animals had been digging in the snow for forage. Then we scooted out of there through the woods to the edge of the field. We stood for a moment, waiting for a cloud to cover the moon, then we broke for it. I took a quick look up at the boys' lodging. The light was moving through the window again. If whoever it was took a look out they'd be bound to see us running across the snowfield in that full moonlight. Between running and being scared and worried, by the time we came to the mill I was soaked with sweat again. We ducked around the corner into the shadows, and stood there panting and catching our breaths. Then we headed for our beds. I was feeling mighty good because I was going to get my revenge on Mr. Hoggart.

Chapter
THIRTEEN

THE NEXT EVENING I walked home with Hetty. "I got to tell your pa something," I said.

"What is it, Annie?"

"You'll learn soon enough," I said.

We went into the house. Mrs. Brown was in the parlor at her spinning wheel, spinning yarn. "Ma," Hetty said, "Annie wants to talk to Pa."

"He's busy now. What's it about, Annie?"

"I've got the proof that Mr. Hoggart's been stealing wool."

She gave me a long look. Then she shook her head. "Annie, you're only going to get yourself in a lot of trouble."

"Ma'am, I'll do anything to get even with him."

She stopped spinning, got up from the wheel, and put her arm around me. "I know," she said. "I know how bad you feel. But we have to let the dead bury the dead. You cannot mourn Robert forever, Annie. You must get on with your life."

"Ma'am, I know you're bound to be right about that, but I just can't get it out of my head. It keeps going around and around inside there, and I can't forget."

She sighed. "Well, you can talk to Mr. Brown. He'll tell you the same. Hetty, go get your pa."

Hetty went out the back to the shop where Mr. Brown was working, and in about a minute the two of them came back. "What's all this, Annie?" Mr. Brown said.

"Sir, me and one of the boys from the mill went into that cabin. We saw the wool."

"Hold it, Annie. What cabin?"

"The one I told you about before. The one out in the woods where Mr. Hoggart's been hiding the wool he steals."

He thought about it for a minute. "I remember now. You said you'd seen the cabin."

"I saw the cabin, and I knew Mr. Hoggart was in it, because I heard noises inside."

" 'Noises' could have been anything, Annie. A raccoon will get in anywhere. So will a skunk."

"It was him, sir. I heard the door open, and I ran, and a few minutes later I saw him come out of the woods into the field."

He nodded. "And you went back there again? That was mighty foolish, Annie. It was a great risk."

"I know. But I had to do it. This time we got inside, and—"

"We? Who's we?"

"One of the New York boys went with me to

help. Mr. Hoggart beat him awful once—kicked him and broke his ribs. We went in. The whole cabin is full of wool." I was skinning mighty near to a lie, for I hadn't gone in myself, and I hadn't seen that wool with my own eyes. But I knew if I said I hadn't seen the wool myself, Mr. Brown wouldn't take it any more serious than he did the first time.

"The place was full of wool?"

"Bags of it." I wished now I'd got Tom to count them. "At least twenty bags," I said.

Mr. Brown pulled at his chin, and thought for a minute. Then he said, "Annie, don't you think you just ought to forget about all of this? What Mr. Hoggart's doing out there in that cabin is between him and Colonel Humphreys."

"I know, sir. I know I ought to mind my own business and stay out of it. But I can't."

He sighed just the way Mrs. Brown had done, and I knew what was coming. "Annie, sometimes it's better to let the dead bury the dead."

Pa had said it first, then Mrs. Brown, and he was the third. "I wished I could, sir, but I can't. It won't stop going around in my head."

He looked at me. "I suppose you think I ought to go to Colonel Humphreys about it."

"He'd be grateful to know, wouldn't he?"

Mr. Brown thought. "I don't know as he would. Mr. Hoggart's got things running smooth at the mill. Colonel Humphreys might be just as happy not to be told about it. You can't tell about these things. I know that twenty bags of wool sounds like a lot, but maybe Colonel Humphreys wouldn't see it that way."

"Sir, if he's got twenty bags out there now, how many more has he sold off before?"

"That's true," he said. "It might come out to a considerable amount. But even so, Colonel Humphreys might see it as a cheap price to pay for a good overseer."

It was all making me feel worried and low in my mind. I'd taken all those risks, and gone to all that trouble, and it didn't mean anything. "Isn't there anything I can do, sir?"

"Annie, my advice is the same as it was; put the whole thing out of your mind. In time you may be able to persuade your pa to let you leave the mill. He's not a bad man. It's just that he's got money worries at the moment."

"Pa's always going to have money worries. It's his way."

"Oh, let's not look on the dark side of it, Annie. Sometimes people change. Maybe this business of the merino ram has taught him a lesson."

"Yes, sir," I said. He sounded just like Hetty. There wasn't any point in arguing with him anymore. He'd clean made up his mind, and that was the end of it. I could understand it all well enough. What it came down to was that nobody wanted to make a fuss. Not Pa, not Mr. Brown, and probably not anybody else. Accusing Mr. Hoggart of stealing was going to cause a lot of people trouble, and ev-

erybody would just as soon let things lie. But not
me. Try as I might to forget about it, I couldn't, for
it made my insides squirm and squiggle. How could
I forget about something that made me feel like that?

What if Mr. Brown was wrong about Colonel
Humphreys? What if Colonel Humphreys would be
glad to know that Mr. Hoggart was stealing wool?
Why, he might even know that wool was missing,
and was wondering who was stealing it. You
couldn't tell. How did Mr. Brown know? He was
just guessing, same as me.

Suppose I wrote Colonel Humphreys a letter.
Suppose I carried it over to his house, and told the
servants it was from Mr. Hoggart. The servants
wouldn't dare open it; they'd take it to Colonel
Humphreys right away. And then we'd see what
happened.

It was mighty risky, for if Mr. Hoggart found
out I knew about the wool, and had told Colonel
Humphreys about it, Mr. Hoggart was sure to do
something serious to me. But I wouldn't sign the
letter. How would anybody know where it had
come from?

So the next night I took a sheet of paper from
Pa's supply, and when it was time to feed the chickens, I carried the piece of paper under my cloak out
to the barn. The chickens were clucking all around
me. I threw them their corn, so they'd leave me
alone for a while. Then I sat on a pile of hay, using a
barrel top as a table, and wrote.

Dear Colonel Humphreys,
Mr. Hoggart has been stealing wool from the
mill. He takes it out of the carding room and
hides it in a little cabin out in the middle of
the woodlot behind the mill. There is a lot of
wool in there now. I saw it.
Your friend.

Of course, that was a lie about seeing the wool,
for I hadn't seen it. But Tom Thrush had seen it. Or
at least he'd said he'd seen it. He wouldn't have lied
about that, would he? Why would he have said
there was wool in there if there wasn't?

I folded the letter up, put it under my cloak,
broke the ice on the chickens' water, and went back
into the house.

The next morning I told Ma I'd be late getting
home from work, because Hetty Brown wanted me
to see her new bonnet. But after work, instead of
going to Hetty's, I set off in the other direction,
heading through the village toward Colonel Humphreys' big house on the hill.

I was feeling mighty nervous. It was bold for
an ordinary mill hand like me, who wasn't anything
but a plain farmer's daughter, to go to somebody as
big and important as Colonel Humphreys; and it was
worse to tell on somebody like Mr. Hoggart. But I
was going to do it, no matter how nervous it made
me feel.

I went through the village, past the green with
the church in the middle and the houses around.

From there you could see Colonel Humphreys' house set on top of the hill, a big square shape with lights burning in the windows, for, of course, Colonel Humphreys was rich and didn't care how many candles he burnt. On I went, until I came to the long drive that ran up the hill through a line of elm trees. I took a deep breath, and started up the driveway. It was good and dark now, and cold, and the stars blinking overhead looked cold too.

At the top of the hill the driveway circled around behind the house, so that deliveries and such could be brought around back to the kitchen, the barns, or the storerooms. I walked around back, wondering if anybody was looking out a window at me. Then I got to the kitchen door. Through the kitchen window I could see the big fireplace. A big piece of beef was on a spit in front of it. The cook was at the table, rolling out some dough for biscuits.

I knocked. In a minute a servant came to the door, his sleeves rolled up, eating the leg of a chicken. He stared down at me, like I was dirt. "Yes, miss?"

"I have a letter for Colonel Humphreys."

The man put out his hand. "Give it to me."

I took it out from under my cloak. "It's important," I said. "It's from Mr. Hoggart—"

"Just give it to me. I'm eating my supper."

I handed it over. All I could do was hope that he didn't lose it, or put it down someplace where it would get chicken gravy or something on it. He shut the door, and I turned and went back around the house, and then down the long driveway. And I'd got down to near the bottom when I heard running footsteps and somebody shout, "Hey, you."

A flash of fear went through me, and I started to run.

"Hey, blame you, hold still," the voice shouted. "Colonel Humphreys wants to see you."

I stopped running, and turned around. The serving man was trotting down the drive. "Blame you, girl, you've made me work up a dreadful sweat. What did you start running for?"

"You scared me," I said.

"Well, I'll scare you good if you do it again. Come back to the house. The colonel's waiting. I'm like to catch my death out here without a coat on."

We went on back to the house, and this time I went in through the front door. There was a hall there, with stairs in front leading to the second floor. I'd never been in such a fancy place in my life— paintings of old-fashioned people on the walls, a tall clock, a glass chandelier with ever so many candles in it winking and shining, a beautiful carpet on the floor. "You wait here," the servant said, and went off. I stood waiting, feeling nervous as could be, for I'd never talked to anybody as important as Colonel Humphreys. I waited for five minutes by the clock, and then the colonel came. He was a tall man with silver hair and a fancy blue jacket on.

He stood for a moment looking at me. "What's your name, miss?" he said.

I didn't want to tell him, for I wanted it to be a

secret who wrote the letter, but, of course, I had to. "Annie Steele, sir."

"Oh, yes," he said. "I know your people. Your father has a farm east of the village, doesn't he? Near where the Bronson boy lived?"

I wished he hadn't mentioned Robert. "Yes, sir. We were friends."

"I see. It must have been hard for you when he died in that accident."

"It wasn't any acci—yes, sir, it was hard for us all."

He reached in his pocket and took out my letter. "Who wrote this? Did you?"

I didn't want to admit it. I wished I could say that somebody else did, and gave it to me to deliver, but, of course, I couldn't, because he'd only ask me who gave it to me. "I did, sir."

He looked down at me some more. It was making me feel mighty small. "Why did you think it was any of your business to meddle in such a thing?"

I blushed. "I—I don't know, sir. I thought you would want to know."

He tapped the letter on his hand, thinking. "And you saw Mr. Hoggart yourself taking wool out of the mill?"

I was feeling mighty hot and sweaty, for he was getting me in a corner. "I didn't see him taking it out, but I saw him packing it into bags."

"How did that come about?"

"It was an accident, sir. I stayed at the mill after

work to ask him not to dock my—to ask him something, and when I went up to the carding room to see him, he was packing wool into some bags."

He gave me a look. "What gave you the right to conclude he was stealing the wool? Certainly he could have had a perfectly good reason for what he was doing?"

"Yes, sir. I mean, no, sir. We already knew he was stealing."

"Who's we?"

I was getting into it far more than I wanted to. "Robert Bronson and me, sir. Robert was tally boy, and he'd known for a long time that Mr. Hoggart was taking wool, because the figures didn't come out right."

"What made him conclude it was Mr. Hoggart?"

"We figured it had to be him. Nobody else had the same chance to do it that he had."

He stood there tapping the letter on his hand, his silver hair glinting a little from the candles in the chandelier over his head. Then he said, "And this cabin—where is it?"

"Out in the middle of the woodlot behind the mill. You can't see it unless you go into the woods. It looks like an ordinary tool shed."

"And you say there's a lot of wool in there?"

"Yes, sir. Bags of it."

He looked at me steady. "You saw it—you saw that wool with your own eyes?"

I was sweating pretty hard now. But I'd said in the letter that I'd seen it. "Yes, sir."

"How did you get into the cabin? Surely it was locked."

"Yes, sir. There's a big lock on the door. We dug under the wall, and skidded in that way."

"Who's we? Your friend Robert?"

I was making a mess of it, all right. "One of the New York boys. I don't know his right name. They call him Jack."

"Jack? About half the boys are called Jack." He thought some more. "You've gone to an awful lot of trouble over this, Annie. What on earth for?"

I could feel the tears come up. "Because of what he did to Robert. That wasn't any accident, sir. He put Robert up on that wheel knowing what would happen. He killed Robert on purpose, because Robert knew he was stealing wool."

He frowned, and shook his head. "That's a hard accusation, Annie."

"I know it, sir. But it's true."

"So you were out for revenge. That isn't very Christian."

"It wasn't very Christian to send Robert up on the waterwheel with that bad foot, either."

"No, I suppose not. *If* that's true." He tapped the letter some more. "All right, Annie. You can go along."

So I skedaddled out of there as fast as I could, mighty glad to be gone, and went on home.

Chapter
FOURTEEN

WELL, THERE WASN'T ANY WAY I could find out what Colonel Humphreys would do about it, or even if he would do anything at all. Maybe it was like Mr. Brown had said—Colonel Humphreys was satisfied with the way Mr. Hoggart was running things, and didn't mind if he was stealing some wool. All I could do was watch and see what happened. Who knew? We might all come to work one day and find that Mr. Hoggart was gone and we had another overseer in his place. I waited, day by day, but nothing happened.

I was thinking about this a few days later, when Tom Thrush came through the slubbing billy room with his broom. I got one look at him and my heart jumped, for his left eye was black and swollen, and there was a big bruise on his other cheek. He pretended to sweep over to me and when he got close said, "I got to talk to you. Slip out at dinnertime."

So I did. I went on out to the slubbing room

and down the stairs. Tom was waiting for me there. "He knows something," he said.

"What happened?"

"He beat the daylights out of me last night. Somebody saw us coming across the field after we was in the cabin, and told him."

"Did they recognize me?"

"No. Leastwise, it didn't seem like. They knew it was me, for the one who told him saw me come in all muddy that night. Maybe they don't know it was you with me."

I felt bad, because I'd practically forced him to go to the cabin and now he'd got a beating for it. "I'm sorry, Tom. I wished I hadn't got you into such trouble."

"It doesn't matter, Miss Annie. I been beat often enough and am used to it." The whole thing worried me, though. Mr. Hoggart was onto something.

"What did you tell him we were doing out there?"

"Oh, something."

That worried me. "You didn't tell him we were in the cabin, did you?"

"I wouldn't do nothing like that, Annie. I ain't that much of a fool."

I tried to look him in the eye. "You're sure?"

"Annie, I ain't that much of a fool."

I was good and worried, now. Had Mr. Hoggart figured out anything? There were a lot of questions I couldn't answer. But my letter to Colonel

Humphreys hadn't done any good. "Tom, I think we'd better be ready to run away. There's no telling what's likely to happen. We'd better be ready to go like a shot. But I'll need some boys' clothes as quick as you can get them. Try to do it right away. Then we'll be ready, no matter what happens."

The next day, just before the five o'clock bell, Tom Thrush came along with his broom and gave me a wink and a nod. Hetty couldn't miss it as she stood right next to me. "He's real uppity, now, isn't he?" she said. But I knew that he was telling me to wait till after all the girls had gone.

The five o'clock bell rang, and the noise of the machinery stopping rumbled through the mill as the boys down below disengaged the gears from the wheel. The girls put on their coats and scarves and filed out. I put on my coat and started down the stairs. Halfway down I said, "Oh, Hetty, I left my scarf behind. Go along. I'm going back for it." She clumped on down, and I heard her footsteps go on outside. I went back into the slubbing room to wait for Tom.

Pretty soon he came in, carrying a lamp and wearing a hat with a wide brim, and walking in a funny, stiff way, like he was having trouble bending his knees.

"I got 'em for you, Miss Annie," he said in a low voice.

I didn't see any package. "Where?"

He took the hat off. "Here," he said.

I swept my hair up over my head and jammed

the hat on top to keep my hair hid. It felt mighty peculiar. I'd worn bonnets all my life, and wasn't used to a hat like that. "How do I look?" I said.

He squinted at me. "Well, you don't look no different to me. But I knows you. I don't doubt you'd look like a boy to somebody else."

I went over to the windows and tried to see my reflection in them, but there was still some light outside and the glass wouldn't reflect except a little. Then I saw Mr. Hoggart down below. I jumped back from the window. I didn't think he'd seen me; I hoped he hadn't, anyway. But I decided we'd better not waste any time getting out of there. "Tom, where are the trousers?"

He pointed to his legs. "I got 'em on underneath. I got on two pair."

"Let me have them, quick," I said. "I saw Mr. Hoggart going by. We must get out of here."

"I got to strip down," he said.

"I'll turn my back. Do it quick." So I turned around, faced the other way, and stood there listening to the sounds of cloth sliding over cloth, and Tom grunting. "Are you almost finished?"

"Most nearly."

Then there was a loud bang of a door, as loud as a gunshot. I jumped around. Mr. Hoggart was standing at the door. He was crouched a little, his arms out, like he was ready to leap. "What's this?" he shouted. "What's going on with you two?"

Tom ducked back, his eyes wide, his mouth open, licking his lips. He was holding the second pair of trousers in his hand. "It wasn't nothin', sir. We was just a-talkin'."

Mr. Hoggart took two steps into the room, and swung his arm, palm open. He caught Tom on the side of his face, and Tom tumbled backward onto the floor. He twisted over onto his hands and knees, and looked upward at Mr. Hoggart, like a dog. "We wasn't doin' nothin', sir."

Mr. Hoggart gave him a quick look. Then he kicked him under the ribs, flipping Tom over on his back. Tom screamed.

"Get out of here, you dirty little pig," Mr. Hoggart shouted. "Get, before I beat the living guts out of you."

I looked around for something to fight him off with. Leaning up against a wall was a heavy iron rod they used for levering up the machinery when they had to make repairs. I wondered if I could get to it before he grabbed me. "Please," I said. "We weren't doing anything."

Mr. Hoggart turned back to me, and stood in the middle of the room, looking at me. Tom was crouched on the floor behind him, holding his chest, and staring upward at Mr. Hoggart, his face all twisted up. Mr. Hoggart reached into the pocket of his coat, and took out a piece of paper, a pen, and a little flask of ink with a stopper in the top. "Now, miss," he said. "You're going to write a little note just the way I tell you to. And if you don't, I'm going to fix you and your little friend here in a way you'll never forget."

I didn't understand what that was all about. "Please. We weren't doing anything."

"Oh, no," he snarled. "Oh, no, not doing anything. Just creeping around places you don't belong in, and meddling in matters that aren't any of your business. You think I don't know who sent Colonel Humphreys that letter?"

I went cold. How had he found out? "What letter, sir? I don't know anything about any letter."

"Don't give me that story. My good friend the footman told me it was you who brought the letter."

I didn't say anything. There wasn't anything to say.

"You're mighty quiet, aren't you? Well, I tell you, you've got good reason to be quiet. Colonel Humphreys was all set to go have a look in that shack where you were nosing around. But I got to him first, miss. Yes, I did. I told him a few things about the trouble you've made around here. He'll never believe another word you say."

I felt sick. So that was what happened. But still, there was nothing to say.

"Now," he said. "You're going to write a nice note saying it was all a lie." He held out the pen.

I didn't move.

"Take it," he said harshly. "Take it and start writing what I tell you."

I couldn't move. I stood there frozen.

"Quickly."

Finally I reached out and took the pen.

"Here," he said furiously, rattling the paper. "Write what I tell you." He laid the piece of paper on the top of the slubbing billy. "Quickly." He held out the flask of ink. I took another quick look at the iron rod. He stepped toward me until his face was right in mine. "Take it," he shouted. He pushed the flask of ink into my hand. "Now, write. Say, 'It was all a lie about there being wool in the cabin.'"

I took the pen, and dipped it into the ink. But I couldn't start writing. My hand just wouldn't move.

"Write it," he shouted. "'It was all a lie about there being wool in the cabin. I made it up to get revenge for Robert's death.' Write that."

The picture of Robert's limp body, with his bones all broken, his foot twisted around backward, and the water freezing on his face came into my mind. "I can't," I whispered. "Not after what you did to Robert." The pen dropped out of my fingers.

He grabbed me by the front of my gown, jerked me toward him, and slammed me on the side of my head. I went dizzy and started to lose track of things. "Write it," he shouted. He bent down, scooped up the pen, and shoved it into my hand, and closed my fingers around it.

I was still feeling dizzy, but I shook my head. He began to shake me back and forth, and then he raised his hand to smack me again. I didn't know where I was anymore. I heard myself shouting, "Help, help!" He hit me on the mouth and I tasted blood. Still holding the front of my gown, he pulled his arm back and I tried to cry out, but no sound came.

And just then there came a thump, like a rock dropping on another rock. Mr. Hoggart's hand came off my gown, and he fell backward onto the floor. Standing behind him, his breath coming and going fast as a machine, was Tom. He had the iron rod raised up over Mr. Hoggart.

Mr. Hoggart was lying on his back, his arms flung out to the sides. There was a bloody patch on the side of his head. He was breathing loud, his eyes closed.

"Don't hit him again, Tom," I shouted. "You'll kill him."

"I aim to, Miss Annie."

"No," I shouted. He lowered the rod so one end was resting on the ground, but he kept it ready in case Mr. Hoggart suddenly came out of it. I knelt down beside him and felt his heart. It was going mighty quick, but it was going. Then, suddenly, I thought of something: Maybe he had the key to the shack in his pocket. I didn't like touching him any more than I had to, but there wasn't any help for it. I slid my hand in one of his trouser pockets. There was nothing there but a handkerchief.

"You looking for his money?" Tom said.

"No. The key. I wouldn't touch his money." I slid my hand in his other pocket. There was stuff in it.

"Well, if you ain't going to touch it, I don't

suppose you'd mind if I done it, then. It ain't often I get the chance to touch any."

I closed my fingers, pulled the stuff out, and dumped it on the ground. There was a small folding knife, a handful of coins, and a key. My heart jumped. "This has to be it, Tom. Come on, let's go." I leapt up, and as I did so Tom dove down, and snatched up the coins and the knife.

"Tom, we shouldn't steal."

"Oh, I wouldn't think of it. But somebody else mightn't be so reliable, and would make off with them coins. So it would be for the best if I hung onto them for safekeeping." And he jammed the coins into his pocket.

Then we raced on out of there and down the long flight of stairs. When we reached the bottom I started off for the snowy field, heading for the woods. And I hadn't got more than three steps when I realized Tom wasn't following me. I stopped and looked back. Tom was standing at the bottom of the steps, looking after me. "Come on, Tom," I shouted.

He stood there for a moment, and then he shook his head. "No, Miss Annie," he said. "I had about enough of that old shack. I had about enough of this here mill too. I think I'm just going to go on down the road as quick as I can, before Mr. Hoggart wakes up. For he's bound to kill me if he catches me. I've got a few shillings in my pocket now, and that'll get me on a boat back down to New York. So, if you don't mind, I'll just say good-bye."

Well, he was right. No matter what the outcome, Mr. Hoggart was bound to beat the whey out of Tom when he came around, and kill him like as not. I jumped back over to him, and gave him a little hug. Then I said, "You'd better get going, Tom, before he wakes up."

"If you ever get to New York, look me up. I'll be on the dock somewhere, like as not." Then he turned, and hobbled off as fast as he could, with his sore ribs.

I didn't wait to see him go, but turned and ran across the snowy field, now all chopped up with tracks, and into the woods. I charged through the woods as fast as I could go, until I came to the cabin. Quickly I slipped the key in the lock and unsnapped it. I took the lock off the door, and shoved it in my pocket. Then I opened the door, and looked in. It was pretty dark inside, but I didn't have any trouble making out the bags of wool, a couple of dozen of them. I shut the door, and then I began to run through the woods, across the snowy field, past the mill, and down the mill road.

When I came to the village road I turned to look around. There was still no sign of Mr. Hoggart. But he'd be on his feet again pretty soon. All I could do was hope he didn't head for the cabin right away. He'd go back to his house and fix himself up first. Or maybe head for a doctor, to sew him up. Even if he did go out to the cabin, it would take him a while to get the wool out of there. He'd have to harness a horse to a wagon, drag the wool from the cabin to the edge of the woods, and load the wagon.

And he wouldn't want to do that in broad daylight, either. He'd wait until nightfall. So I had some time.

I turned onto the village road, and trotted along it until I came to our farm lane. I turned down it; but instead of heading on home, I jumped over the stone wall into the field where the merino ram was grazing, and headed out for the woodlot. In about five minutes I began to hear the sound of George's bucksaw going *zizz, zizz, zizz,* as steady as anything. I reached the woodlot; there, a little way in, was George, in the middle of a clearing with stumps all around him, and a big pile of firewood in a heap behind him. He was bent over a log, pulling the saw, and didn't hear me come up until I was right next to him. Then he stopped sawing and straightened up. "Annie? What are you doing here?" Then he looked at my face. "What on earth happened to you?"

"He hit me. I wrote a letter to Colonel Humphreys that he was stealing wool. Mr. Hoggart found out, and he hit me." Suddenly I began to cry, for it was all too much for me. And sobbing away like that, I told him the whole story—how we'd slipped into the cabin and found the wool, writing the letter to Colonel Humphreys, and everything else. Finally I got finished and wiped the tears off my face with my shirt. Then I said, "I can't go back to the mill, George. I just can't, I can't. I'll have to run away instead."

George stood there, still holding the bucksaw,

looking grim. Then he said, "Come on, let's go see that cabin."

"What are you going to do, George?"

"Don't you worry, Annie. I'm going to fix that man Hoggart so he'll wish he never heard of Humphreysville." He began to walk off as fast as he could go, so I had to jog to keep up with him. We cut across the field, past that blame merino ram that had caused so much trouble, onto the farm lane, out to the village road and then along to the mill road. George never stopped walking with those long strides, never looked around, never said anything. He just kept on going.

We turned into the mill road, went out past the mill, and across the snowy field all chewed up with muddy footprints. When we came to the edge of the woods George stopped. "It's in there?"

"About fifty yards, maybe."

"Go on. You know where it is. Lead the way."

So I set off through the woods, my heart beating fast, for I was scared that Mr. Hoggart might be there. But I knew that with George behind me, there wasn't anything he could do to me anymore. I pushed on through the woods, and in a minute I began to see the shape of the cabin dimly through the trees. I stopped. "That's it," I said.

George pushed past me, and began to stride forward. I followed him, and in about five seconds I noticed that the door wasn't open anymore. It was closed. Then I heard a low curse, and I saw through the branches that Mr. Hoggart was standing in front of the door, bent over doing something. George began to sprint, ducking and dodging through the trees, and I began to run after him.

Now Mr. Hoggart heard us. He straightened up and looked around. George went plunging toward him. "You," he shouted.

Mr. Hoggart had tied a handkerchief around his head where Tom Thrush had whacked him, but I could still see a patch of dried blood on his cheek. "What are you doing here? Who are you?" Then he noticed me. "Not you again. Oh, are you in for—"

Then George grabbed him by his shirtfront. He raised his head. "Hoggart, if you ever touch that girl again I'm going to split your head open for good and all."

"Listen, you—" But George was bigger and stronger, for he'd spent his life cutting wood.

George swung his hand around. It made a great slapping noise when it hit. Mr. Hoggart's head jerked back. "Don't," he gasped out.

"George," I shouted. "He's put a new lock on the door."

George gave Mr. Hoggart a shake, and then he looked at the door. "See if it's closed, Annie."

I jumped over to the door and pulled on the lock. "It's closed," I said.

George gave Mr. Hoggart another shake. "I want the key."

"Let go of me," Mr. Hoggart gasped again.

George began to twist the other man's collar. "No. No," said Mr. Hoggart.

"The key."

"No. Don't." He began to choke.

"The key."

Suddenly, Mr. Hoggart reached into his pocket and drew out a key. George snatched it from his hand. Then he flung Mr. Hoggart away like an old sack of corn husks. Mr. Hoggart fell to the ground and lay there, his hands around his neck, groaning. George leapt to the cabin door, turned the key in the lock, pulled off the lock, and swung the door open. He whistled. "Wool, all right. Plenty of it too."

Then I noticed that Mr. Hoggart was up on his knees and crawling off through the woods. "George, he's getting away."

"Let him go," George said. "It doesn't matter what he does anymore. He's finished around here. We'll go see Colonel Humphreys. Once he sees this wool he'll come to realize that you were the one telling the truth, and Hoggart was the liar. I think he'll believe your story now."

I looked at him. "George, what's going to happen to me?"

He stood there, holding the lock in his hand, and thinking. "Well, there's Pa's debts to consider. I think what we'd best do is tell him straight out that unless he works out something, we'll leave—you and me. Pa isn't a bad man, but he's got the weakness for things. He'll come around."

"And he'll take back the things he bought? The clock and the saddle and such?"

"The saddle, anyway. He hasn't got any use for

it until he gets a horse. But maybe we ought to let him keep the clock. Times *are* changing, Annie. There's going to be more mills, and more people coming in from the farms to work on them. You can't stop progress, if that's what you want to call it."

"And I won't have to work in the mill anymore, George?"

"I'm not sure, Annie. I think maybe you might have to, for a little while. And I'll have to go on cutting firewood. For a while, until we can whittle down Pa's debt some. Just a few months more, I think. Then I guess you can start back to school."

"That's all I ever wanted," I said.

"I think it'll come, Annie. Now, let's go see Colonel Humphreys."

We started off through the woods. "George," I said. "Why did everything have to change? Why couldn't they go on the way they always did?"

"Things change, Annie."

"Is it better?"

He shrugged. "I don't know, Annie. I guess you'll have to decide that for yourself."

How Much of This Story Is True?

The Clock IS A MADE-UP STORY—
the fiction part of this historical novel. Annie and
her family came right out of our imaginations, and
so did Robert and Mr. Hoggart. We made up all the
particular events in this story. Nevertheless, it is
true-to-life in every way.

Colonel Humphreys really existed. In 1806 he
established the first real factory in Connecticut, a
woolen textile mill just as described here. He
brought in about 150 orphans from New York to
work in it, and after introducing the slubbing billies,
he was the first mill owner in Connecticut to hire
girls.

Colonel Humphreys also, in 1802, was the first
to import merino sheep into the United States. These
sheep had very long wool, which was easier to work
with and made better fabric than any other. At first
the merinos were worth hundreds of dollars, but
later, when others were brought to America by the
scores, the price suddenly fell, and many men who

had invested in them when the price was high lost great sums of money, just like Annie's father.

Mr. Hoggart represents the kind of overseer that, unfortunately, was too often found in these early mills. As we studied early industrial history, we found many episodes of unbelievably cruel behavior by overseers, some leading to the deaths of mill-workers. One young boy committed suicide rather than go back to the mill. The way in which Robert died was a very likely happenstance. Our own ancestor, Samuel Slater, was crippled as a result of chopping ice off a waterwheel.

Although the story is made up, it is based on real conditions and real events that you can study in good history books. Though most people welcomed the coming of mills to their towns, just as most Americans today are enthusiastic about computer development and space exploration, many people began to wonder if the new industrial life in new cities was any better than the old farm life in the country. And about a generation after the mill came to Humphreysville, people like Ralph Waldo Emerson, whom we quote on the opening page of this book, began to wonder if it was really worth giving up control over one's own time and life in order to have so many material possessions. We have written this book to give you some help in thinking about whether "progress" is always for the better.

JAMES LINCOLN COLLIER is the coauthor, with his brother, Christopher Collier, of *My Brother Sam Is Dead,* a Newbery Honor Book; *The Bloody Country; The Winter Hero; Who Is Carrie?; War Comes to Willy Freeman;* and *Jump Ship to Freedom.* He has written many other highly acclaimed books for young readers, including *The Teddy Bear Habit* and, for adults, *The Making of Jazz.* He lives in New York City.

CHRISTOPHER COLLIER is a professor of history at the University of Connecticut and Connecticut State Historian. His field is early American history, especially the American Revolution. He is the author of *Roger Sherman's Connecticut: Yankee Politics and the American Revolution* and other works. He and his family live in Orange, Connecticut.